P9-ELR-447

MANYWHERE

MCD
FARRAR, STRAUS AND GIROUX
NEW YORK

MANYWHERE

- STORIES -

MORGAN THOMAS

MCD
Farrar, Straus and Giroux
120 Broadway, New York 10271

Copyright © 2022 by Morgan Thomas
All rights reserved
Printed in the United States of America
First edition, 2022

These stories previously appeared, in slightly different form, in the following publications: *them.* ("Taylor Johnson's Lightning Man"), *Joyland* ("That Drowning Place"), *American Short Fiction* ("Transit"), *The Atlantic* ("Bump"), *Electric Literature* ("Alta's Place"), the *Kenyon Review* online ("The Expectation of Cooper Hill"), *StoryQuarterly* ("Surrogate"), and the *Kenyon Review* ("Manywhere").

Bird on title-page spread by PinkPueblo / shutterstock.com.

Library of Congress Cataloging-in-Publication Data
Names: Thomas, Morgan, 1992– author.
Title: Manywhere : stories / Morgan Thomas.
Description: First edition. | New York : MCD / Farrar, Straus and Giroux, 2022.
Identifiers: LCCN 2021040911 | ISBN 9780374602482 (hardcover)
Subjects: LCSH: Gender nonconformity—Fiction. | LCGFT: Short stories.
Classification: LCC PS3620.H6353 M36 2022 | DDC 813/.6—dc23
LC record available at https://lccn.loc.gov/2021040911

Designed by Janet Evans-Scanlon

Our books may be purchased in bulk for promotional, educational, or business use. Please contact your local bookseller or the Macmillan Corporate and Premium Sales Department at 1-800-221-7945, extension 5442, or by email at MacmillanSpecialMarkets@macmillan.com.

www.mcdbooks.com • www.fsgbooks.com
Follow us on Twitter, Facebook, and Instagram at @mcdbooks

10 9 8 7 6 5 4 3 2 1

For Bea, who introduced me to Frank,
and for anyone who's gone looking for
themself in the archives

Contents

—

MANYWHERE

TAYLOR JOHNSON'S
LIGHTNING MAN

—•—

October, 2008. I'm here in the photo booth on Ellis Island, waiting for you, lightning man.

You're sailing from London on the ocean liner *New York*. Your ship docks in one hour, one hundred years ago. We'll miss each other by a century, I know. It doesn't matter to me. I'm here anyway, waiting. I have something to tell you.

After you disembark, follow signs to the gift shop. I'm on the first floor, near the water fountains, past the ladies'. Make a right at the elevator. The medical ward where you spent most of your time on the island is closed to visitors now. The room where you argued your case before the Board of Special Inquiry is locked, visible only through glass windows. But the site where you had your photograph taken on Ellis Island is open to tourists, marked by a photo booth. There is still one camera on Ellis Island, and I'm sitting in front of it. I'll meet you here.

I'm wearing a homburg with a stiff brim and a suit just like yours. The tourists mistake me for a living exhibit, a reenactor. "Who are you?" they ask me. I tell them to guess.

I came up on the train, two days spent on the rails you once rode the other way. This morning, I told my mother I was taking a ferry to Ellis Island. She said, "We didn't come that way. It was Canal Street for us."

"I know."

"There's no one up there for you," she said, hanging up.

But I haven't come looking for family. I've come to meet you, lightning man.

> As this is the lightning-rod season, it is the opportune time to put the homeowner on his guard against the wiles of one lightning-rod man, who is now going his rounds in the lower wards equipped with a "reel" of twisted white "ribbon," some alleged insulators, a few gilded points and spikes, and an enormous quantity of impudent loquacity.
>
> —*The Louisiana Electrical Review,*
> *January 30, 1909*

You protected us from fires.

My mother invoked you when the weather turned, when hard rain shorted our window units, when jellyfish sucked up into Gulf Power's turbines fried the circuitry and we lived for days in the dark. When the generator at the corner of Lee and Empire blew, when the neighbor girl dropped her hair dryer into the kitchen sink and the surge protectors tripped one after another down the row of flats, my mother said, "Where's that lightning man?"

When a storm tracked off the Gulf to New Orleans, she didn't call on Jesus. She clasped her hands in front of the standing fan, and she said, "Hear us, lightning man." We climbed into the bathtub, put the mattress there on top and hunched against it for breathing room. We listened to shingles pull away from the roof, to the trees outside popping like cans, to the Keasey family next door singing "Hosanna," crammed into their tub same as us. We said, "Come on, lightning man. Knock at our door, lightning man. Keep us safe, lightning man. We're calling you."

After, in the giddy, permissive days following any storm, I used bungee cords for jump ropes. I skipped with the other kids, singing, "Lightning man, lightning man, where's your rod?" We tapped coastguardsmen on the shoulder to whisper the question and ran shrieking. We couldn't have said why it was funny, but we were certain it was.

We made our own lightning rods. We lashed coat hangers to the gutter. We tied Christmas ornaments to brooms with butcher's twine and dangled them out windows. If the ornament twisted left, a storm was coming. If it twisted right, our mamas were.

We all knew your story. We'd heard it from our mothers over dinners of macaroni eaten before the standing fans. The year was 1920. You appeared in a thunderstorm on the porch of the landlord's flat. You held a staff of iron from which hung a crystal ball, the sort used for divination. You knocked. The landlord mistook your knocking for thunder. Perhaps your knocking was thunder. You let the thunder do your knocking for you.

You sold lightning rods, iron rods. A dollar a foot. The glass balls you'd throw in free. Four rods would cover the flats, protect them from lightning fires. Forty feet of iron. Forty dollars.

The landlord refused. The landlord was warted, pimpled, bespectacled, every kind of ugly. The landlord was tight as a mule's ass with his money.

One year later, the flats caught fire. Inside, twenty-four people. Women and children. Four rods would have covered the flats. Forty dollars.

Most ended the story there, with a suck of air through their teeth, one shake of the head. "We may be stingy, but we ain't cheap."

Not my mother. My mother went on.

You died in 1932, she said. You were entombed in St. Louis Cemetery No. 3, east of New Orleans. The undertaker, when he stripped your body for embalming, discovered you had been all along a woman costumed with a man's suit and a smoker's cough, a Canadian with no U.S. citizenship and no family to speak of.

My mother liked your story because she thought it illustrated the progress made by women of her generation. "These days, you wouldn't have to hide that way. You could sell a lightning rod wearing a skirt. Might sell more that way." I liked your story because I suspected even then you weren't a woman or a man. You were a lightning man with a knock like thunder. I felt close to you.

The other mothers called their children away when my mother started talking about the lightning man. "You're making things up," they said. They disapproved of my mother. They disapproved of her flat chest. Twelve years ago, a doctor took my mother's breasts. Medicare covered her surgery, but they wouldn't pay for implants. Implants were cosmetic, they said. My mother didn't mind, claimed she looked younger without the jugs and felt lighter besides. She walked around in denim cutoffs and sleeveless tops with Hello Kitty screen prints, which left the skin of her midriff bare. Going flat, she called it, like pop left too long in the sun.

"You'd do better with a pair of gel forms," the other women told her when she went out in a dress that hung lower in the front than it was meant to hang. "You'd do better with two balls of newspaper and a nursing bra."

My mother ignored these suggestions, disdained conformity of any sort. Don't wear pumps, she told me, they'll ruin your feet. Don't wear makeup, it'll ruin your skin. If you own a car, you should know how to fix one. Don't rely on anybody outside yourself for anything, and especially not on a man.

When I was fourteen a doctor told me if I wanted my period I'd have to eat more. I'd have to turn myself into a woman if it was a woman I wanted to be. Driving home from that appointment, I boasted to my mother, "I'm too thin to be a woman."

"Don't be ridiculous," she said. "You're as much a woman as I am." For my mother, *woman* was a word as vast and inescapable as ocean. It encompassed anything. Nothing I did—not binding or wearing boxers or finding an outboard motor on the road and hauling it home—could shake her conception of me. This was the freedom she offered.

I ate less after the doctor's appointment. I didn't want to turn myself into anything. When my breasts and hips swelled, I ran them off the way my mother ran off any man looking to lay her down without making a home for her. I swam off the levees in boys' trunks. I kept my body slim. Stock, like water boiled over bone. I figured you, lightning man, had done the same.

We both prayed to you. When the wind picked up, my mother put her hands together, the knobs of her thumbs pressed against her lips—"Don't let me down, lightning man." I prayed for other things. I prayed you were real. I prayed I would find you.

This is the history of an honest, industrious woman, an enlisted soldier in the army of labor, who found herself almost hopelessly handicapped by a lack of female attractiveness and encumbered with a man's mustache, fighting for fifteen years a losing battle. Then, as her only alternative, she dons male attire, smoothing pleasantly and profitably the rough road ahead of her.

—*"Trousered Woman Arrives at Ellis Island,"*
Los Angeles Times, *October 12, 1908*

I searched for years. I looked in my middle school history books, in St. Louis Cemetery, in the records of the New Orleans Historical Society. You weren't there. I found you finally at the Louisiana State Capitol. Your story and photo sat side by side within a brochure for Ellis Island. The History Center at Ellis Island was exhibiting the portraits of Augustus Sherman—chief registry clerk, inveterate bachelor, amateur photographer. Augustus Sherman photographed the detained—those waiting for travel tickets, for money, for approval from the Board of Special Inquiry, for the male relative without whom an unmarried woman could not enter the country.

He photographed an Italian seamstress, her hair braided into a crest at her scalp.

An Italian bagpiper. A Romanian shepherd.

Dutch children, boy and girl. Three Dutch women.

Three Slovakian women.

Three Georgian Cossacks, employed by the Buffalo Bill Wild West Show.

Three women from Guadeloupe, en route to Canada.

Eleven Romanians, Gypsies, all deported.

One German stowaway, his nude torso adorned with tattoos, deported.

Eleazar Kaminetzko, twenty-six, Russian, Hebrew, SS *Hamburg*. Vegetarian.

Vladek Cyganiewicz Zbyszko, strongman, posing on a black wooden stool, one fist at his temple, one fist at his lower back.

Mary Johnson, fifty, came as Frank Woodhull, October 4, 1908, dressed fifteen years in men's clothes.

There you were.

Frank Woodhull—Rakish in a slouch hat. Stolid. Broad-shouldered. Gray about the temples. Blessed with a mustache, a low-toned voice, size nine feet, and rheumatism, which caused your knuckles to swell and stiffen. Men's hands, the papers praised you.

Frank Woodhull—Protestant, Acadian, Canadian, moneyed. You were easy for them to love.

And they did. "A desirable immigrant." "Blameless." "Law-abiding." "Adopted men's clothes to get on in the world." "Able, by adopting men's dress, to live a clean, respectable, and independent life." "Dresses as a man to find honest occupation." "Refined and somewhat cultured in her manner." "An alien, but not an undesirable one." "A testament to strength of mind and determination near superhuman."

> Women have a hard time in this world. They are walking advertisements for the milliner, the dry goods stores, the jewelers, and other shops. They live in the main only for their clothes, and now and then when a woman comes to the front who does not care for dress she is looked upon as a freak and a crank. With me how different. See this hat? I've worn this hat for three years, and it cost me just three dollars. What woman could have worn a hat so long?
>
> —*"Mustached, She Plays Man,"*
> New York Sun, *October 11, 1908*

My mother knows her own mind, same as you.

Last year, the Plaquemines Parish Support for Survivors Society gave my mother one thousand dollars toward the cost of implants. She took that money to Hell or High Water Tattoos, along with a print of Audubon's—"Bunting, Painted; 1827." She paid the artist to ink the buntings there on her chest. It took twelve hours, three sessions, fifteen hundred dollars. She lay on her back with her eyes closed while the artist with her needle detailed one branch of a fruiting persimmon tree and four birds in different stages of feeding or flight.

After her third session, my mother came home brimming. One scar was now the undercurve of a bird's wing, the other a lip of shadow cupping a ripe persimmon.

I asked her—"Can I take your photo?"

"What would you want to do that for?" she said, but I thought, from the flush of her cheeks, that she was flattered.

I took her portrait with an old Kodak Brownie, developed it in Tupperware baths in the narrow toilet room of our apartment, submitted it to Nikon's Emerging Photographers contest. It won second place. They want to print it in their winter magazine, one full glossy page. I told her. I thought she'd be pleased.

"I didn't know you'd sold it," she said.

"I didn't sell it. I submitted it. I want people to see it, to see you."

"People see me all the time. See me at the grocery store. See me pumping gas."

"That's not what I mean."

"You can withdraw it, I guess. Tell them you've changed your mind."

"Why would I withdraw it?"

"Because I'm asking you to. What's this about, Taylor? Is it about getting a little certificate? Is it about getting your name in

11

a magazine? I thought I'd raised you better than selling out for those things."

"How am I selling out?"

"It's not decent. That sort of photo. Imagine if someone saw it, someone I knew, someone's kids."

"It's perfectly decent. It's beautiful." And I still think so.

In her portrait, my mother stands by the window, the dining table behind her laden with sausage and toast. I positioned her there. I wanted the light coming at a slant over her chest and her stomach. I wanted her topless, which she was. I didn't want her arms folded across her chest, but she folded them, suddenly shy, deepening the habitual hunch of her shoulders.

"You about done?" she'd said.

"Just about."

I waited. I waited until she let her arms go slack, fall to her sides. I let the shutter fall at the same time.

In my mother's portrait, you cannot see her face. Only her chin tipped toward the window lets you know she's looking out. Not her legs, her wide bare feet. Not her denim shorts, but her hip bones are there. Her stomach, with its faint center scar. The cereal-bowl cavity of her chest. She is the backdrop against which the birds appear, still blurry, still inflamed in places, lifted slightly as though trying to pull away from her skin.

"If that photo isn't decent to you, I don't want to know what you think of me," I said. I often wandered the apartment in nothing but board shorts. I hadn't thought decency was anything we cared about.

"You clean up fine when you try, Taylor. We both do. I'd have cleaned up for the photo if I knew you were going to be sharing it."

"Are you ashamed of it? Of who you are, who I am?"

"Don't make this about you."

But I felt the panicked jolt of a missed step, a missed stop, of looking up from dancing at a bar to find the music's off and the lights are dim and I am fully alone. "I'd be grateful. If someone took a photo of me, I'd be grateful."

"We've got plenty of photos of you."

"Not good ones." In photos, I'm awkward—skinny as sticks with my shoulders thrown back, my eyes bugged for the camera. Unrecognizable. What wouldn't I give for someone to take a photo of me, all unsuspecting, and show it to me later, saying, "Look how lovely you are"? What wouldn't I give to stumble across a photo of myself in a magazine or a gallery or staring up from a newspaper stand and realize, stunned, that it's me? "Everyone loves the photo," I said.

"I don't want it printed, end of conversation."

"What if Frank Woodhull had said that to Augustus Sherman? What if Frank Woodhull hadn't wanted any portraits printed, and Sherman had agreed?"

"Who?"

"Frank Woodhull. The lightning man."

"What does this have to do with the lightning man?"

"That photo of Frank inspired me, inspired lots of people."

"You think my portrait will inspire a generation? To what, tattoo their tits?"

"I'm just saying Frank probably had no choice, and that's awful, but without that photo where would I be?"

"You'd be wherever you want to be."

But I wouldn't be here now, on Ellis Island, walking through the TSA-style precheck, complete with body scans. I wouldn't be leaning over the railing of the stairs, where on this day in 1908 the doctors watched you climb from the baggage room. All the passengers from steerage were funneled up those stairs. Two at a time. In 1908, they pulled aside the boy with hiccups, the man with a limp, the woman with a swollen belly, and you. You were slight of build for a man. Perhaps tubercular. Kept overnight in a private matron's room, because you could not be trusted with the women, could not be trusted with the men.

By morning, they'd declared you healthy. They let you walk into the city by yourself, free as a man. By morning, your photo was in the paper, front page. You'd done it. You walked onto the island suspected of tuberculosis and perversion besides, then walked off a day later with your belongings and your dignity and every paper singing your praises.

I'd have stuck around for praise like that, but you fled. You chartered a lobster boat to New Jersey and took the Morgan rails from there, made for the Big Easy, where what's printed in a New York paper has no more relevance than the weather in Chicago, stock options in Alaskan oil, San Francisco sun.

I've planned and planned for this day. Every other day in your life is a mystery to me, but I know how you spent October 8. For years, I've prepared my re-creation of it.

When you arrive, we'll sit together in the photo booth. We

won't eat the café food. Mountain Dew. Broccoli cheddar soup in a toss-away bowl. Weak tea. Stewed prunes on dry bread. Ground dog sausage and rye heels. Overpriced, inedible in any century. We'll sit with sandwiches I packed this morning, and we'll talk until you're comfortable, Frank Woodhull, until the camera, if it took our photo, would catch the two of us together, laughing like any pair of friends.

You can tell me why you fled New York City. Was it really so awful, Frank Woodhull, to be praised like that?

I gave my occupation as canvasser, but I have done many things. I've sold books, lightning rods, and toiletries. I've worked in stores. Now I go to New Orleans where there are chances of employment.

—*"Officials Find There Is No Law Under Which Mary Johnson Could Be Deported,"* The New York Times, *October 7, 1908*

The photo booth is automatic. Electric! Photo me too! Take your own portraits. Four poses for three dollars. Two-minute exposure to print time. I sit on a stool of green plastic, which is too small to be comfortable. The floor is black-and-white tile, checkerboard.

"What are you doing in there?" the tourists ask me. They're impatient. "Haven't you been in there long enough?"

I tell them I'm waiting for someone.

What if I don't recognize you? What if you draw back the

curtain, and with the light in my eyes I don't see it's you? What if you're not wearing your hat? Your hair on top might have more gray than I expected. You might have replaced your patent leather loafers with wooden clogs. You might have removed your spectacles. I might think you're just another tourist come to ogle the exam rooms at Ellis Island.

"Pardon," you'll say.

"I'm waiting for someone," I'll say. "I'll be out of your way soon."

"It's pressing," you'll say. You'll be agitated. Your shirt will bunch in the waist of your pants, where you tucked it hastily. You'll have come from the matron's room, where you disrobed and sat for ages in a hospital gown, waiting for the doctor to come and pinch and prod and hammer and hum and declare you a woman, then ratchet up the lid of your eye with a buttonhook and drop tuberculin onto the sclera to check for any reaction, any infection. I'll study your eyes, but there won't be any swelling. You're lucky, Frank Woodhull.

"I need the booth," you'll say. "They've asked me to sit for a photo."

I'll realize then. I'll realize it's you. I'll leap from my seat as if it's electric.

"It's a pleasure," I'll say, extending my hand. After a moment, you'll take it. "Mr. Woodhull," I'll say. "It's a pleasure to meet you."

We'll trade places. I'll exit the photo booth, and you'll take a seat. You'll remove your glasses. "No hats," you say. "No spectacles, I was told by the clerk."

"You need quarters," I say. I want to be helpful. "Three dollars' worth."

"Three dollars?" You are outraged. "That's a day's wages. This hat cost me three dollars, and it's custom made from lambswool."

I read about that hat in the *New York Sun*. I don't say this. I stay quiet as you dig in your pocket for quarters. I know you don't have a choice but to take this photo, and you know it, too.

You drop the coins singly into the slot. You're one quarter short. "They nickel and dime you. They always have."

I lend you a quarter.

You study the photo booth. "What will it do? What does it do to a person?"

"It takes your photo. Four photos."

"Four? I'll be hours."

"It's quick," I say.

"It's an outrage. For all the bluster of this country, I never expected to be hauled out on the carpet over my clothes." Another quarter rings into the slot. "I'm not a lawbreaker. I seek only a life of independence and freedom."

Which sounds nice, Frank Woodhull, but you fed the same line to the *Times*.

"Does it bother you? Someone taking your photo?"

"Bother? Only two things in this land bother me—lightning and bluebottle flies. Lightning will kill you, and those flies bite."

"What if it was in the newspapers?"

"You won't see me in the papers."

"But if you were."

"Mine's a life best lived in private," you say, which is something my mother would say. For a moment, I'm worried you might feel as she felt about having your photo in the paper—angry, humiliated, your secret shared without permission.

"What if everyone loved the photo, though? Wouldn't you be glad?"

"My only philosophy with a newspaper is this: buy for a penny, sell for a dime."

"It wouldn't scare you, though. It wouldn't make you ashamed like it did my mother."

"Only two things scare me—lightning and bluebottle flies. Lightning will—"

"Should I withdraw the photo of my mother?"

"I'm afraid I haven't made your mother's acquaintance. She's a fine woman, I'm sure."

She is, Frank Woodhull. That's it exactly.

You straighten your collar, pull your shoulders back, preparing. "It'll be quick, you said? I'd rather it's not drawn out."

"It's quick."

You insert the final quarter, and the machine flashes four times. You screech like a cat doused in water, blow through the curtain. "God damn," you say. "It's a lightning machine. You never said it was a lightning machine."

"It's not dangerous."

"I could have been electrocuted. I could have died. They're trying to kill me."

"They love you," I say.

I take the strip of photos from the feeder. The first photo is as it should be—you face the camera, square. You're missing only your homburg and your spectacles. In the second photo, your chin looks toward the curtain, your hands guard your face from the flashes. The third shows only your right shoulder in one corner, fleeing. The last is blank.

"I'm terrified of lightning. All my life, I've avoided lightning."

I study the first, nearly perfect photo. "How did you do it?"

Don't touch the window latch in a storm, you tell me. Don't stand on the hearth. Avoid pine trees. Avoid lonely barns. Avoid running water and crowds of men. Men are the best conductors. Lightning goes through and through a man, but only peels a tree.

I've read Melville, too, Frank Woodhull. I know about lightning. I know getting lightning struck is, more than anything, a matter of tremendous bad luck. You've been lucky, Frank Woodhull. That's all. Maybe luck, too, got you through Ellis Island. You can't tell me. You can't tell me anything I don't already know.

I'll show you how to work the photo booth. There's nothing to it. It's even fun, Frank Woodhull, and you'll come to see that, too. I'll position you on the squat green stool with the light coming in from above, so it doesn't flash off your spectacles. I'll suggest you wear your homburg and spectacles, and you'll agree you don't look like yourself without them. I'll show you how to shift your pose, so the next flash catches a different angle, how to raise one eyebrow, how to show your teeth. I have plenty of quarters.

We'll take one with your head above mine, stacked like grapefruit. One with the two of us facing as if in a mirror. I'll let you take a strip alone. We'll ring quarters into the slot until we're ankle deep in photo strips, until they're rolling from the booth out into the carriage room, into the gift shop, and we're laughing.

Let's keep going, Frank Woodhull. Let's take photos for days.

But they're waiting for you upstairs, the Board of Special Inquiry. Of course, you'll have to bring them a photo. You choose one of the good, familiar photos. In it, you sit in your hat and spectacles, facing the camera, your head tilted just a little to the right, your mouth a firm, flat line.

"At the risk of saying too much," I say, "I'm a fan of that photo. Everything I am is because of that photo."

"This photo? The photo we took not a quarter hour ago?"

"Do you like it?"

"It serves the purpose," you say, but I think, from the lift of your lips, you're satisfied. I knew you'd like it, Frank Woodhull. I knew I could rely on you.

Go now, or you'll be late for your hearing. I'll clean up the photos we've left behind. I'll sort through them on my hands and knees, looking for another one in which you face the camera directly, shoulders square, your homburg and spectacles combining to obscure your eyes. One in which you are exactly, perfectly as you should be. I hope you'll forgive me, Frank Woodhull, if I share that photo with a few people, maybe with a magazine. You said yourself it wouldn't bother you, and I don't mean it as any sort of betrayal. I have to share it, because, Frank Woodhull, I'm in it, too.

THAT DROWNING PLACE

—

Driving north on the island road, they were mostly innocent. They'd done awful things, but the sort of awful that from a distance looks like resourcefulness and might even—at a seafood boil, in a certain crowd, after several drinks—offer some allure. One worked as an attorney for the oil company responsible for the Deepwater Horizon spill. One sold her child's baby teeth, wiggling them loose prematurely with her thumbs. One raced oil trains on the mainland for dare money, her siblings shouting encouragement from the truck bed. In the last race, right as she crossed the tracks, her younger sister, Lena, bounced from the truck bed onto the track and was sliced into three by the train. Heading north, they thought they'd left those things behind them. On the island road, they drove like fishermen, fast enough through the standing water to leave a double V wake, sounding the horn as if on a gillnetter in the Gulf.

They left for better fishing. *Reeled in a snapper the other day with four balls. I'm not eating anything with more balls than I have.* For better weather. For better pay. They left because the flood insurance man refused to renew. *He said we should think about relocating. I told him the only thing I want to relocate is your jawbone.* They left because the dunes were bald, sand fleas the only life on the beaches. Because the road went under with every tide, and one day it was going under for good. They left trees with salt-encrusted roots. They left car frames rusted through by the warm, wet brine. They left the boxing club and stadium, which had never been used. They left the ground broken for an indoor ice-skating rink, the last in a series of projects designed to make their town too valuable to abandon. *We made sure we didn't look poor. You look poor, they'll treat you poor.* They left their best bird dog clipped to a high line in the backyard. They left the Easter crockery. Lena's sister left Lena's bed unmade, as Lena had left it. She left the skirt onto which Lena had sewn eight hundred sequins. She left the bowl from which Lena had eaten her cereal the morning she died, the milk hardened at the bottom to a gray plaque.

What did Lena's sister take? Two things: Lena's driver's license with the thumbnail photo. Lena's name. Lena's photo looked more like her than her own did. She thought it was little enough to take. She thought Lena would stay behind.

Four-wheelers on flatbeds. Gooseneck trailers stacked with rolls of barbed wire. Carpets with spores of black mold burred in the shag. *Danamarie* and *Salty Mare* and *Y-Knot*. Six meat rabbits in a rusted hutch. A refrigerator with no door. Trap buoys painted in the family colors, bouncing up into the wind like flags. American flags. In the cab, three kids and a dog. A crib mattress yellowed with urine. A wide-wheeled racing chair. Four bottles of Southern Comfort. An oxygen tank. One Ruger 10/22 Sporter

Camo Exclusive. A Glock Gen4. A breast pump. Vicodin. An inflatable pool. A duck decoy, carved from cedar. Holy water. A Fisher-Price Stroll & Learn. Mud boots and mudbugs and ice in a foam cooler and insulin and gasoline. All they could carry from the houses left behind them. The houses themselves, they carried in pieces—sheet metal and planks of hard pine and two-paned windows wrapped carefully in shoe paper—from which they planned to rebuild.

In those trucks, above the beat of air through the windows and the drawl of the radio, they talked about the land awaiting them. They'd printed grainy images from Google Earth of the plots parceled from an old sugar plantation and assigned to them in order by last name. *Quarter acre backs up to a creek. Got an outbuilding already. Got a slope to it.* They thumbed through copies of *Architectural Digest* and circled photos of stone-floored basements and game rooms large enough to fit two pool tables. They studied an old Kodak photograph of the shotgun house their great-grandfather built at the turn of the century, which they planned to replicate right down to the square-head screws. They talked about how to stretch the settlement they'd gotten for the stilt-houses they were leaving behind. They imagined his-and-hers bedrooms and dormer windows with pillowed seats and frescoed mantels and tire swings. Lena—she'd taken that name, it was her name now—imagined a room to herself and a bed draped in tulle. They all imagined dancing late into the night on a wrap-around porch. They imagined rivers so thick with crawfish you could scoop up a meal in a bucket, fingers of the Gulf tumbling north, fresh and potable.

Maybe no one had told them about us. Maybe they believed the land they'd been promised to be virginal—a green and empty paradise. Maybe they chose to forget us. Maybe they believed if they refused to think of us, we would disappear.

They stopped only when absolutely necessary. To refuel. To tighten the cables securing mattress to roof rack. To squat in the reeds, tennis shoes on the asphalt, and shit. Loose, watery shits. Giardia in the water, according to the EPA, which some believed and some thought was a trick to get them to take the settlement the government offered. One stopped to take a leak, leaving their water behind in the water. Lena stopped to cast fry nets, which sunk through silt and grew heavy with fish. One stopped to shoot a night heron for their dinner. *Most birds, you need a twelve-gauge, but you can drop a night heron with dust.* One, who stopped to plug their bleeding with a dry tampon, looked back at the island where an osprey pair circled a nesting tree. *For a second it looked like it used to. The island was green, green, green.*

Ninety-three miles north, we waited for them. We held a parade for them, to advertise our goodwill. We wore face masks made of stiffened gauze, adorned with deep-set wrinkles and antlers. We brought out our best float from the year's Mardi Gras—a dragon sculpted from wound wrap. We brought out our best fiddler. Our best wagon. We brought out our replica of the Sears Tower, assembled from Coke bottles we couldn't return. We brought the hand-cranked wheelchair we'd engineered with bicycle chains. We draped a banner—"Hello Islanders"—across the back of the chair. We held signs—"Refugees welcome." They honked. They waved. Their children flattened their faces against the windows. They slowed for directions to their plots. They slowed so we could check the pressure of their right, front tire. They slowed to throw a red slushy out of the car window, splattering the hems of our trousers. *We're not refugees. We're Americans.* They stopped to shake our hands. They stopped to quiet their kids, who were clamoring to see us up close. They stopped to ask if there were more of us. We shook our heads. We numbered only sixteen. They numbered sixty-nine. They said they guessed we'd be seeing an awful lot of each other. When their kids stuck their owlish heads out the rear windows, they said, *Get back in the goddamn car.* They gave us corn bread. They gave us business cards. They gave us the finger. They sped past us without seeming to see us at all.

That first night, in their FEMA trailers, they slept on thin cots with metal frames. They dreamed of riding mowers clipping blankets of zoysia. They dreamed of the cremated body they'd left on the island, dreamed a strong, nowhere wind that tore the roof from their house and slurped the ashes up into the sky. They dreamed of Lena's severed legs dancing salsa in black hose with terrible runs. They dreamed the storm followed them here, and the trailer floated off on the waves, and they heard their oldest daughter gasping for breath, choking as the waves curled over her head, and they sat up, still half asleep, slapping the wall where the light switch would have been if this was really their wall, their house. Their daughter sobbed in the next cot. They lay back again on their cot, which others had used before them, which smelled like the untold tragedies of other people. They turned their back. *I'm trying to sleep.* That first night, they drank. They smudged with sage. They fisted, fucked just for the familiarity of it. They woke every fifteen minutes to spin the handle on the crank lantern, so it wouldn't dim and die. They lit three candles to the Virgin, the Mother, and the Beloved, asked for a blessing on this new land. They slept alone for the first time in decades, better than ever before. That first night, they woke up at four in the morning and walked out into the yard, where they saw us move through our lit bedrooms—most of us sleep fitfully, if at all—and they wondered what we were doing and if we were watching them.

We learned how not to call them. Not rednecks. Not white trash. They were Cajun—descended from the Canadian Acadians, who were put on a boat for New England in 1759 and traveled overland from there to the Louisiana colony. *This isn't our first go-round. We've been forced out before.*

They learned how not to call us. Not lepers. Not cripples. Not contagious, not even those of us with tight-fisted hands or dimpled faces. We had Hansen's disease, well under control in every one of us. We were barbers and journalists and engineers. We had an American Legion, a Mexican Club, a softball league. We sang choir and visited the school in Baton Rouge and stocked the freshest shrimp north of the bayou in our market. Some of us were American. All of us were Louisianan. We were the daughters of Ukrainian bankers, nieces of British smugglers, descendants of a German armadillo farmer, a Texan hog mogul, a Korean diplomat, come to the National Hansen's Disease Clinical Center for the gold-standard treatment.

Things between us were mostly ordinary. Early on, they came to us for water, their plots having no pipes. They came to us for news. They came to us for seafood, because our crabs were freshest, our shrimp wild caught. Some came to us with decks of cards, and we played gin rummy elbow to elbow, pausing between hands to pour drinks. They drank beer. We drank Bloody Marys, because gluten inflamed the disease. They kept their thumbnails long to cheat. We said, "Baby, be there," for luck, before every draw. They came with stories. They told us about standing chest-deep in waders in a redfish pond as a water moccasin slicked past, towing an alligator three times its size. They told us about the spill. Most of them had worked it, one way or another—built booms or run skimmers. One had his boat pressed into service for the cleanup. *I told them they might as well take my legs, but they only needed the boat.* One had tried to outrun a plane spraying Corexit. He'd motored his skiff full throttle, watching the golden, chemical rain sweep the Gulf until it was on him. *Burned my eyes worse than Mace. And I know Mace.* They told us the man they'd married had been known as the Cajun Fisherman. *Best fishing guide on the island, he was. Up here, what is he?* They told us all the ways they'd tried to keep the water back from their front porch. All the ways you could fish panfish. All the ways you could run a dragnet. All the ways you could rear a kid wrong.

Lena was the only one who came to us for comfort. She told

us how her sister had looked on the train tracks on her hands and knees—like a dog. She told us how she had taken her sister's name and felt, sometimes, the chill of carrying the name of someone dead. We understood. We also carried the names of the dead. One of us, the story goes, had died in a knife fight in Croatia. Another at the Bay of Pigs. Our families held funerals with empty caskets and forgot us. Lena showed us her sister's license with the thumbnail photo. "You look just like her," we said. Early on, we told them what they wanted to hear. We matched them drink for drink, story for story. We told them about the evening we got the jukebox running in the cafeteria and two-stepped until dawn. We told them about our Fat Tuesday, when we showered the citizens of Carville with armadillo doubloons. We told them about the Saturday afternoons when our daughter came to see us, smuggled in beneath the seat of a Lincoln Continental. Children weren't allowed onto the grounds, and we weren't allowed off the grounds back then. We told them of the narrow moon nights when we snuck quiet and calm through the garden and the gap in the fence to fish in the river or spend a night over liquor in Baton Rouge or visit family in Puerto Rico. We told them the ugly stories. Two days locked in a sleeping compartment on the Amtrak Sunset on our way to the Home—food brought in on a plastic tray, piss taken away in plastic bottles, not allowed to leave. We told them we couldn't have children anymore. We'd been sterilized by the disease, by the knife, by time. The ones like us who came after us, who caught the disease now from their brother or an armadillo, would never wrap their ulcered feet in moleskin, wouldn't have to forego handshakes. They could walk in a crowd undetected. We were the last ones who'd live apart. We were dying out. These days, we could go home if we wanted to. We could leave anytime. No one would stop us. We stayed, because we preferred it here, in the home we'd made for ourselves. Once, Lena tried to refuse a story. It was a private story—just Lena and one of us in a third-floor room in the Home. We tried to tell her of the rainstorm that saved our house. Our first house, in Galveston. It was one week after we left for the Home. The neighbors found out where we'd gone. They learned we had the disease. They thought we might have left something behind in the carpet or the linens that was catching, so they plugged bottles of gasoline with rags and lit them and tossed them through the windows of the house where we'd lived. The corner of the sunroom caught first, one little gleam before the flame scampered mouselike along the floorboards. Our wife was inside, and she came awake beneath a flat layer of smoke, already coughing, and she—Lena stopped us there with a hand on our arm. *I'm tired. Maybe in the morning, you can finish.* But we were sunk deep in memory. We saw the flames reach the roof. We saw them jig down the beams. We saw our wife in the bed we'd shared, not moving, not leaping from the bed, not making for the door. She lay as if still sleeping, making up her mind. We saw the fire truck rolling reluctantly—no lights, no sirens—up the gravel road. We saw the sparks spit from the curtains, seeding small fires in the floor. We saw our wife rise—weary and annoyed, as she often was of a morning—and walk through the small flames that pitted the floor out into the yard, burning her left foot so badly the entire sole later peeled away in one piece. We looked up then, and we saw Lena scrunched in the hand-crank chair, rolling it a little forward, a little back, her eyes fixed on the window—not looking through it. Looking at the glass. We apologized to her. We held her and promised not to tell her those things again. Privately, we thought she should be stronger.

Many of them came to us for construction supplies. We sold the supplies at a discount, because it was clear they'd expected the check they were cut by the government to go further than it did. *Laid a sewage line, and I'm broke.* One painted a dove in flight on a glass window and traded it to us for three months of groceries. That window is still up in our chapel. Some came to us for loans. Some hired on construction workers from companies out of Florida and Tennessee. People who knew how to square a corner, how to brace a deck, took to sitting on the concrete walls around the Home on Monday mornings, waiting to get hired on for the week. They never came to us for advice, but we found ways to offer it. We printed the plans we'd drawn up for our houses, bound them and shelved them at our library for easy reference. They didn't reference them. We told them as we scanned their groceries that they didn't need to build on pilings. They built up anyway. *Water's always coming. You can't hide from the water forever.* One built a house with a domed roof. *For wind protection.* One built a house entirely of rubber tires. One walled off the bathroom in glass, so you could see them moving from toilet to tub, a dark curve. Lena's father planned two bedrooms, which was what he could afford, though Lena begged for a room to herself. One planned a second-floor porch, then cut it to cut costs and now has just the door, swinging out onto nothing. One was struck in the head by a falling beam and died. One built the frame for the house they'd always wanted and ran out of money and hanged themself from the rafters. Their partner put the lot up for sale, buried a statue of St. Joseph head-down in the yard, and went south again. One built an exact replica of the house they'd had on the island, hung the same photos, drew a waterline in blue pen on every wall. One dug for a basement like the ones in the *Digest*. They hit water, of course. *Underneath, it's just like the island, same goddamn water, same goddamn place.* Most built beyond their means. We resented their extravagance. Our houses were two-room boxes of various colors, which we'd built ourselves from spare lumber and scrap metal. Few had a bathroom. Fewer still a kitchen. The doctors hadn't wanted us cooking for ourselves. All our lives, we'd fried stolen eggs, used old license plates for pans. We could still be overcome by the intimacy of a saucepan brought to a private simmer. We thought them spoiled, entitled as children. Some of them built nothing, simply continued living in their FEMA trailers, their things piling up in the yard, and we disliked them most of all.

In the center of their plots, they wanted a replica of Easy Street, complete with facades for Stein's Cleaners, the Jazz Café, the Fatty Shack, and a jetty extending out into the trees. They built just the jetty before they ran out of scrap wood and nails. Not even a full jetty—a stub of a jetty, resting on the grass. They sat out there dawn until dusk with coolers open and empty at their feet. They invited us to join them, but direct sun inflamed the disease. As we passed with our parasols, headed to the grocery or headed to the Home, we asked them, "What are you doing out there?" They said they were fishing. *We talk. We laugh. We catch trout*. But the boats they'd hauled up from the island sat on trailers in the corners of their lots, yellowing in the sun. In the evenings, they would stagger home beneath the weight of their tackle gear and ice. We put up a "Now Hiring" sign at the grocery, though we didn't need more hands. They didn't apply. In the privacy of the clinic yard, we began to call them lazy.

We gave them honey sticks. We gave them gumdrop tomatoes from our garden plots. We gave them two schoolrooms in the lowest floor of the Home, so they wouldn't have to bus their kids into town. They taught classes in French and wasted Wednesday mornings on the Bible. We said nothing. We couldn't give them everything they wanted. They wanted to use the tennis courts, but our knees were no good for tennis. For years we'd used the courts for shuffleboard. Some of them wanted their own church, named after an obscure saint, but there was only one priest willing to come out weekly from Baton Rouge and no sense building more houses of God than you had men to shake their fists in them. Some of them wanted to print their own newspaper on our presses, but we had an award-winning paper. We didn't need another. We thought they understood this.

We didn't choose favorites, though if we had we'd have chosen Lena. Lena, who was not quite one of them, not quite one of us, who walked from their jetty to our rose garden with such ease you could almost believe, watching her, there was no barrier between us but distance. When others tried to follow her, they found the garden deserted, the museum closed for lunch, our doors shut against them. If they caught us outside, they stammered a greeting and walked past, like they planned to stroll all the way to the city.

They preferred to meet us on the neutral, ritualized grounds of the card tables or the shuffleboard court, where the rules were long-standing. Lena was different. Some said it was because of the age she was when they came here—old enough to know her own mind, but not so old it had gone rigid and brittle as dry clay. Some said it was her sister. They pointed out the day in the Coke bottle garden when Lena caught her reflection in the distorted glass of one bottle and spooked—her breathing too fast, her hands spidering over her face. When we asked her what was wrong, she said, *I saw her.* We understood she meant her sister. We saw figments, sometimes, in the long-unused rooms. We sometimes woke to the smell of link sausage browning in the Home's kitchen, though the power was cut to that kitchen at the turn of the century. Maybe Lena under-stood us on account of losing her sister. Some said Lena was just one of those people oblivious to the niceties of others, as a ghost is oblivious to the distinction between doorway and wall. But Lena was never oblivious. You could tell by her smile, a sly mischievous smile, which she wore when she knelt in the garden beside us—a smile that said she knew she was getting away with something. She pressed her luck. She asked us for her own room in the Home, a place to escape her family and the ghost of her sister. We didn't give her a room. Those rooms had their own ghosts and had to stay shut. Some of us still regret that. Some of us would have shared a room with her if she'd been interested in sharing. One of us told Lena she loved her, a confession Lena received gracefully but with a certain formality, a distance that dissuaded further admissions of that kind. Some of us believe if we'd just given her a room, one room, everything would have come out differently.

When they forgot where they were, we reminded them. When Ricardo spun up off the coast of Senegal, crossed the Atlantic, ricocheted off the Yucatán, and swept up onto the delta, we reminded them they didn't need to board their windows or tie down their patio chairs. They didn't need to stock jugs of water and gasoline, buy extra cartridges for their guns. They didn't need to invest in radios—hams and handhelds with antennas long as a grown man's arm. "We're a hundred miles north of the delta," we reminded them. When they let the faucet run to fill their tubs, in case the lens of groundwater went salty, we reminded them we're on county water. When a boy died of carbon monoxide poisoning from his family's generator, they sent Lena to tell us. *Same thing happened in Rita*, she said. *Happens every storm.* We reminded Lena there was no storm. They hadn't needed the generator. *A boy died*, Lena said. *A boy died—don't you care about that?* But he hadn't died here, we said. He hadn't died in our Home. In our Home, kids didn't die of generators or trains. Only on the island would you hear of a thing like that.

Lena looked at us then like she didn't know us, like we couldn't be trusted to tell a hurricane from a leaky faucet and couldn't be trusted to give a damn. We'd seen that look before. We'd seen it on the faces of the state workers who came monthly to trim our hedges. We'd seen it on the faces of the ones who spent their days out on the jetty. We never expected to see it on Lena's face.

We learned the funeral for the boy would be held in our chapel from a notice on the chapel door. We didn't attend, unsure of our welcome, but we sent two platters of deli sandwiches and a king cake to be neighborly.

Somehow, we never expected them to get old. We never expected them to settle in. We never thought they'd get jobs with the National Guard or the state prison. Never thought they'd get degrees in finance and medicine. Never thought they'd want a quarter share in our grocery store or a voting position on the Friends of the Library board. Never thought they'd get the hip surgery they'd been putting off or sell the boats sun-bleached from years out of water. We never thought Lena would get an assistant realtor job in Baton Rouge, would get insurance to cover the hormones she needed. We never thought she'd be the one to sell the Home, our Home, but she was—sold it for the state, for a 10 percent commission. Lena sold it fast to Sunset Living, the first company that placed a bid. Sunset Living planned to turn it into an assisted-living center for folks from New Orleans. We never expected the lights to flicker on again in the upstairs windows of the Home, but Sunset Living started to renovate. Sunset Living offered us rooms at a discount. They offered to make sure we were comfortable right up until our end. They sent Lena to talk us into it. Lena wanted us to stay. Lena tried to tell us she'd been thinking of us when she sold the Home, tried to tell us the change was what we needed. Lena talked fast and smooth as any salesperson, had the shine of someone who'd found a place for herself. We refused to stay. We would not live again in the too-warm rooms where doctors could enter without knocking whenever they liked. We would not die there. We left. In cars driven by nephews and third cousins. In a coach-class seat on the Amtrak

Sunset. On planes bound for Incheon and Philadelphia. After we left, they sold the gauze masks and the bike-chain chair. They sold the photograph prints of the front corridor for ten dollars apiece on eBay. They sold tours of the Coke bottle garden. They sold our houses. They disinfected them with medical-grade bleach, stripped the carpets and the wallpaper. They sold them as Craftsmans, which they were—every board sawed, every nail pounded, every screw drilled by hand. Once, Lena called us to tell us about the renovations of our homes. We didn't pick up. Lena talked in the message about dormer windows with pillowed seats and frescoed mantels. We recall how she sounded in that message—with a note in her voice like she needed our approval. We called her back, left our own message—"You've done real well for yourself," we said. We imagine Lena replays that message in front of the mirror in her Craftsman home. Sometimes, Lena hears our voice. Sometimes, the voice of her sister. Sometimes, she burns her hair with her straightening iron, and the smell reminds her, for no reason she understands, of us.

This we know to be true: When there's a storm, they tune in to the Weather Channel. They sit before the television. They watch their old home go under, up to its neck in lapping waves. They do not think of us, but as the drones pan over their old island, they bite their cuticles and look for their houses. They say, *Baby, be there*, which we taught them to say. And as we, in doctor's offices in northern cities and countries across the ocean, look at X-rays of dark fluid seeping into our weary, porous lungs, we use their words for acceptance—*You can't hide from the water forever.*

TRANSIT

—

She mistook me for a vampire. It's an easy mistake to make.

I was traveling alone, which no girl would these days. I was pale. I wore black jeans, black T-shirt, black jacket. I'd come from a three-month stint at the Naked House, where parents send kids who refuse seconds, refuse to spread peanut butter on their celery sticks. I'd been expelled from the House, not discharged, so I was still bony and furry, still inclined to refuse roasted sunflower seeds and peanut halves when they were offered, to feed privately in bathroom stalls or crouched by the waste bins.

I was stranded with everyone else in Jubilee, Louisiana, my train delayed by flooding. We'd been stuck for five hours in the SunTran station, where the water fountains were dry, the soda machine out of order. We were all thirsty. It's hard to tell just from looking who's pining for Gatorade, who for liquor, who for blood.

Vampires don't exist, but she was the type to believe—pushing thirty with a streak of purple in her hair and a Fall Out Boy decal on her bag. She entered the SunTran station wearing a bright yellow raincoat, black boots buckled up to her knee. Water from the flooded parking lot rolled over the tile, preceding her.

Generally, I would have avoided her, as I avoided anyone who assumed I desired connection or conversation, but I was newly alone. At the Naked House, I'd had a shower buddy and a home-work group and a dining party. So when she asked if she'd missed the five o'clock, I said, "Hasn't come."

A mistake. She took my words as an invitation to sit beside me. She divulged her home place (Jubilee), her destination (Charleston), and her reason for travel (a friend's wedding, where she would officiate—"Thirty minutes online, and you're ordained," she said).

"What about you?" she asked. "Where are you headed?"

"Anywhere I choose." I said it the way you're supposed to say it, like it's an achievement. I had a ticket to Houston, where my mother lived, but I hadn't expected delays or transfers. I hadn't expected to find myself in the SunTran station in Jubilee, where all was chaos—seats and refreshments and destinations up to anyone's interpretation. No one had told me I'd have to get off the train and back on again. No one had told me I'd have to decide myself to board a train home.

She pulled out a bag of cherry tomatoes and began eating them one by one like popcorn. She offered me one.

That's when I said it—as a tease, for a lark—"I only drink blood." At the Naked House, in the weeks before my expulsion, this was a running joke. We'd read books about vampires, passed them to each other beneath the dining table. The other girls liked the women—pale, thin women who tried and failed to resist their hunger. I liked Petronia. Petronia was angry and made men suck her cock. I'd never read about anyone like her. She hardly bothered to resist feeding. The girls nicknamed me Pet after her, because I also failed to resist. At the dinner table, I always folded first. I was quickest to lift my fork.

This was the context of the joke I told Sarah May Shell, a context she didn't understand. I was no longer at the Naked House. The joke didn't translate. Nothing translated. Sarah's eyes went wide, and she crossed herself, but she didn't move away. "You came to see Mary," she said.

"Who?"

"You're not the first. The Count came by buggy to the grotto daily until the Civil War. Then there was a whole group down from New York in the fifties, came on company time for a sales conference, but also"—she curled her fingers into fangs or maybe quotation marks—"they were hoping Mary could burn the thirst out of them."

"Who's Mary?"

"Mary," she said. "Like from the Bible, Mary. We've got one of our own—Mary in the grotto." She showed me a photo on her phone of a statue in some shallow cave, stone eyes lifted, stone palms pressed together. "The Count commissioned her. The Count was a vampire, too."

"She looks like a man," I said. Something in the bones of her face, the thickness of her fingers.

"Well, the Count had her made in his mother's likeness, and his mother was a man."

Between the stone palms of the statue was a fresh lily and this lily, said Sarah May Shell, was the miracle—every day there was a new one. People said the Count freshened the lily, but by all calculations the Count should have died two hundred years ago.

"I'm a cousin of the Count on my mother's side."

"It was just a joke," I said.

"Plenty like you have tried getting Mary to set them straight."

"I'm not a vampire."

"What do you mean you're not?"

"I've never drunk blood."

She didn't believe me, and I didn't blame her. She'd seen something in me, something real. She alone of the people trapped in that SunTran station understood I was capable of harm. "Well," she said, trying to find some excuse for me, trying to help me out of this trap I'd made for myself, "there's no reason to drink blood if you've never lacked for water."

Sarah May Shell had been thirsty. I could tell from the way she held herself, the way she spoke. She'd seen hard times. She'd maybe drunk her own urine. She'd maybe eaten still-green strawberries for thirst.

"I'm not a vampire," I said again.

"Then what are you?" Sarah May Shell asked me.

At the Naked House, I was bed fourteen, chair six in the blue kitchen, second-to-last in the weighing line, which meant fifteen minutes more sleep than the girl who weighed first. At the Naked House, everyone knew where they stood.

The House had a library, where we were expected to self-educate, to read texts from decades ago. Those books gave us names like flowers—anorexia nervosa, anorexia athletica, anorexia divinica. We read stories of nuns fasting until they saw light and swooned. We read about pituitary hormones and controlling mothers and the patriarchy. Anorexia is the desire to tame animal propensities gone wrong in high-spirited patients. The anorexic does not feel pain like the control. The stick of a pin to the anorexic is only mildly exciting. Causes include a detached insula. Trauma to the lateral cortex. Sensory neurons poorly myelinated.

"We're all thin on myelin," Happy sang. Happy was my best friend at the Naked House. When I cut the skin at her hairline, so she could bloody a maxi pad, Happy said, "Watch out for my insula."

She was just playing.

I said anyway, "Shut up."

I would not have cut Happy Waggoner with an X-Acto knife if it had been up to me. But at the Naked House, three regular periods will get you home. Happy didn't want periods, but she wanted home. So once monthly, she held her hair up from the nape of her neck. She said, "You're the best, Blue," as the parted skin turned first white, then slowly red. I pressed a pad to the slit. Scalp wounds bleed heavy and can be hidden beneath hair, which is why we cut there. At the Naked House, we weighed naked. Otherwise girls would line the hems of their skirts with batteries and bits of metal to trick the scale.

Some days Happy asked me to nick her skin though there was no need to wet a pad. It was important to her, the routine, keeping me in practice. It was important to both of us. She worried it would get harder if left too long, the way a goat's teats wither to a dry bag if she goes unmilked.

Her name was Happy because of the way she laughed—on her back, feet kicking against the orange House carpet. At nothing. Braying. "Like a frog," Briony said once. Too long. If we were in class the tutors asked her to finish in the hall. We sat at our desks while Happy in the hallway threw her body against the walls and made the very floor of the Naked House shake with her laughter. She told me on my second day, "You take yourself too serious, Blue." Laughter, if you really dig into it, is hard on the body. Happy dug in.

Take for instance the day I asked Happy, "Would we date? If we weren't in here."

Happy said, "Slow down, Blue, baby. I'm no lezzo."

"That's not what I mean. I'm not a woman."

"None of us are women," Happy said with a shudder at all the word conjured—menstrual blood and fat and children and fat, the kind of fat you could ball up in your fist.

"If I weren't a girl," I said, "would you date me?"

Happy grinned, and I knew I'd lost her. Happy asked, "If you're not a girl, what are you?" Happy pulled her bottom lip in against her teeth, her incisors poking out long and sharp. "Someving supernatural?"

"I'm whatever. I could be whatever."

Happy didn't hear. She threw back her head and retreated into her laughter.

She was the best of us. She often went days refusing to eat. Once the Matron actually let her go and stopped feeding her through a tube. Happy lasted just ninety-six hours before she came to breakfast. She gulped her juice. She folded hotcakes and swallowed them down without chewing. She kept her eyes on her plate. We watched her, disappointed. We expected more of Happy. We wanted to admire her. She did not even laugh, that morning. If she had laughed, mouth full of buttermilk crumbs, or sprayed juice through her nose onto the tablecloth, we might have forgiven her.

The Matron said to the rest of us, "Eat. Two minutes." We ate. The buttermilk cakes were thick in our mouths. We blamed Happy.

Happy went back, the next day, to refusing her lunches, and the Matron to the feeding tube, but we recognized it now as a game, a tired one. I said to Happy, "You didn't last any longer than my mother with a stomach virus."

She said, "Let's see you try it." I didn't. I understood I would fail. Her laughter sharpened. She was laughing at me.

It was easy then to tell about the maxi pads. After I told, the Matron said, "You're a good friend to Happy Waggoner." She said it easily, like tossing jerky to a well-mannered dog.

The Matron shaved Happy's head the next day, so everyone could see the scars. The Matron checked everyone's scalp. In Briony's thick hair, she found a dozen nails banded to the underlayer for extra weight. She made Briony wear the nails night and day for a week. Briony clinked like a belled cow. She missed a day trip with her father, which she had been promised the month before. She blamed Happy. "Next time you want someone to stick you, ask me," she said. "I won't play around."

But I was the only one Happy asked. She knew I wouldn't try anything she hadn't told me to do. "You're a coward, Blue," she used to say. Happy respected Briony. Happy trusted me.

She learned to tie head scarves. Her mother sent her a hat from Nepal, because bald Happy took chill easily. We all took chill easily. Happy's hair did not grow over the scars, so for weeks they were visible, hideous on her head.

She would come sometimes in the early night and sit with her knees drawn up just beside my bed. "Scratch it, Blue," she would say. Her head itched where the hair was growing in. She knew I didn't like to touch it, to see the back of her neck crease when she lifted her chin.

"I'm not angry you told them," she said once. She pressed back into my hand. If I'd pulled away, she would have knocked her head against the metal rail of my twin. I didn't pull away.

"I didn't tell," I said.

"I'm not angry," Happy said. The bristles of her new-growth hair were sharp against my palm. I wanted to make her angry. I wanted to know I could surprise her.

I was many things at the Naked House. I was Happy Waggoner's best friend.

To Sarah May Shell I made it out like Happy cut herself. "I told on her," I said. "It was best for her I told."

"Sounds rough, kid," she said, the way people do when you've been talking too long.

"I shouldn't have told," I said, asking her again.

Then a voice came over the loudspeaker to say all ground transportation had been canceled for the night. The price of our tickets had been refunded. We should approach the ticket booth for new reservations in the morning.

On the benches, a flurry. Pockets unzipped, bags rifled through, cell phones extracted, whispers and nudges, eyes rolled up to the ceiling in exasperation or in prayer. One woman pulled out her wallet and started a conversation with the ticket seller, who it was clear couldn't do a thing no matter how often the woman snapped and unsnapped her wallet.

"They think there's nothing here," said Sarah May Shell. "They think this isn't any kind of place, just some fog you pass through between where you're from and where you're headed. They can't imagine people live their whole lives here."

"I'd live here."

"Moment I saw you I knew you belonged here. Like the Count belonged."

"Like his mother."

"No, his mother wasn't a vampire. Just an old lawman, sort of man who wore a wig in court. He needed a place to bring up the child he'd had, and he chose Jubilee, because nobody here would run him off."

"Sounds just like me," I said, though I wasn't planning on children, and I hadn't chosen Jubilee, not yet.

At the train station in Houston, my mother waited for me. I hadn't called to tell her I'd be delayed. Last time I talked to my mother, she did the talking. She said she'd got me a train ticket home, said she was disappointed in me. She'd been working double shifts at Planet Vitamin to cover my tuition at the House. She'd rented out my bedroom. She'd bred some of her three-year-old bitches, which is risky, and one had already whelped, the pups smaller than mice, all of them dead. On her off days, she drove to the corner of Main and Independence, where she sat with a sign that said "Christ is Lord," taking money for the church collection bin. When the traffic was slow, she sorted her change, flattened wrinkles from the bills. Sometimes, she slipped a five or ten into the pocket of her coat. I guessed she was relieved she didn't need to find money for the House anymore. I didn't ask if she'd be glad to have me home. She didn't say.

Sarah May Shell didn't call anyone, either. She walked to the counter of the SunTran Bistro and Café, which sold cold pastries and postcards and cat key chains. She ordered two sweet buns for a dollar apiece.

While the man working the bistro wrapped her sweet buns, she asked him, "Is your house dry?"

"We're all right," he said. "We come to expect it—rains in Texas, floods in Jubilee."

"I was telling this one about Mary in the grotto," Sarah May Shell said, waving me over. "I was telling her about the Count bringing a new lily every day for two centuries."

"There's some in this town will tell you anything," the man working the bistro said to me.

"You don't believe it?" said Sarah May Shell.

"The Count was a philanthropist is all. Built the hospital."

"Oldest vampire trick in the book. Every transfusion, you take a little off the top and nobody the wiser."

"What about his mother?" I was more interested in the virgin than the son.

"That one was mean as a snake," said the man working the bistro. "Staked out a piece of marsh when he wasn't much older than you, and he'd shoot a man for looking sideways at one of his oaks. Had over a dozen people brought up on charges of trespassing, then he dies and his son turns the land over to the city anyway. No, I wouldn't call them good people, but they were no vampires."

"They were fine people," Sarah May Shell said. "They belonged here."

As we spoke, the line for the bistro grew until it stretched out the swinging double doors. The people far back in line stood on tiptoe to count sweet buns and soft cookies, to number the almond biscuits. No one wanted to be left choosing between the biscotti and the pecan brittle. They eyed Sarah's sweet buns. There weren't enough sweet buns for everyone. They probably thought it criminal that one person had bought two sweet buns.

"You got that kind of money, you belong anywhere you choose," said the man working the bistro. He called the next person in line. Sarah May Shell offered me a sweet bun.

"No, thanks."

"Of course, you wouldn't," she said, pleased. "How about a smoke?"

I didn't smoke. I said, "Sure."

In the parking lot we stood next to her truck, in water to our ankles. In the bed of her truck there were three crates of green tomatoes and a mattress torn on one corner down to its coil springs.

"You live in this truck?" I asked her.

"Sometimes. She gets me where I want to go."

She lit a cigarette for me, which I held until it went out. "He never knew him," she said. "The Count."

"You never knew him."

"But I'm descended. I know the stories. He doesn't know. He had no idea who he was talking to."

"I'm not a vampire."

"I'm not scared of you. I know you're more likely to be killed by a bus. You're more likely to be attacked by a shark."

"Are you the one with the lilies?"

She shook her head, smiled a little, glad I'd thought her capable. "I would. If I were like you, I would." She kept her eyes on me—a stare so long and unblinking I thought she might be working up the nerve to kiss me. Instead she said, "The Count's son got turned in the city. Went to school in Boston. Came back pale and weak and reclusive." She reached to relight my cigarette, but I handed it back to her. "How'd it happen to you? Your—you know—turn."

"Mom's boyfriend," I said. Startling—how quickly the lie came.

She nodded. "I've heard it's usually someone you know." She put my cigarette between her lips, drew on both at once, so invested in my identity as a vampire it seemed even to me sort of true—not, "Yes, Your Honor," true, but true enough to tell your mother on the phone when there was nothing else to say. "I'm a big admirer. I never thought I'd meet one. Figured you kept apart or were all long gone."

"We're still around," I said. I didn't want to disappoint her. "Did the Count's mother like lilies?"

"He died," she said, as if this eliminated any possible preference. "Mary just looks like him." She offered me a green tomato from the crate in the back of her truck. "Keep you from getting thirsty."

In the Naked House, we got five minutes per fish stick. If you didn't finish your fish sticks or your cheese grits or your orange juice, the Matron would give you the tit, which was protein powder and water. You could swallow it down or take it through a tube. There were some girls would take it again and again. One had convinced her parents to pay to put a port into the wall of her abdomen, because it was getting so it took two tries to tube her. I never had that kind of trouble. I can eat quick. I can drink twelve ounces of orange juice through a straw in sixty seconds. Don't think. Don't breathe. Just pull.

I was used to eating to please an audience. I drained the juice from her tomato as a vampire would, tossed the sapped skin into the water.

People will ask what you want. Do you want hot sauce on your potato thins? Want fries with that? Spicy or mild? Very berry or monkey crunch? Want another? Want to buy one get one? Want to play a game? Want to know a secret? Want to have some fun? Want less hair on your chest? Want more hair on your chin? Want the tit? Want to tattle? Want to pierce your tongue? Want to cut me just once just there? Don't you want that? Don't you? Don't you walk away. Don't you run.

At the Naked House they asked, "Do you want to be here another month?" They asked, "Do you want to help me help you?"

I wanted to be at the Naked House. The other girls all had stories of resistance. Happy's brother threatened to lock her in the dog crate if she wouldn't sit quiet in the car. Briony's mother put NyQuil Nighttime in her cereal milk, and she woke up groggy in bed number nine. Not me. My mother asked me if I wanted to go, and I said yes. Florida seemed exotic, a chance to get away.

In flooded Jubilee, the ones who knew what they wanted drowsed in line, waiting for the stroke of midnight, when tickets went on sale for the day's trains. The first train was to arrive in Jubilee at six o'clock in the morning. It would run from Jubilee to Florida without further delay.

At 12:01, the ones at the head of the line began rapping their knuckles against the Plexiglas window, like trying to wake a bear at the zoo. When the night-shift worker emerged from the break room and spit her gum expertly into the trash can, they cheered.

I waited in line, though the train was eastbound, and I was heading west. At the Naked House, you learned not to skip a line if a line was offered.

Sarah May Shell did not wait in line. She went right to the front. She said to the man next in line, "Is this the train heading east?"

"That's right," the man said.

"Line's back there," said the woman behind him and pointed.

Sarah May Shell did not go to the back of the line. She stood beside the woman, not stepping into the line, not cutting anyone off, not asking anyone for anything. When the teller said, "I'll help the next in line," Sarah May Shell said, "If you'll pardon me," and took her place at the window. No one stopped her doing it.

We shambled forward as the teller called, "Next." Each person put dry lips right up close to the speak-hole and whispered through it Alexandria or Birmingham.

When I got to the counter the woman said to me, "Where is it you're trying to get?"

I said through the metal speak-hole, "It's been busy for you this morning, I can see that." I pressed my lips to the speak-hole. I whispered, "Your house dry?"

"Where to, hon?" She had a fat face, a kind face.

"Have you ever brought a lily to the grotto?"

"Where do you want to go?"

Happy Waggoner went to Cocoa Beach. She left the Naked House one week before I did. She had reached one hundred pounds, which was going-home weight.

I said, "Wherever. Ticket seller's choice."

She said, "You're wasting my time."

The voice came then over the loudspeaker. The ticket seller wasn't expecting it. She lifted her eyes with the rest of us toward the white stippled ceiling. We listened, still as prayer. The train coming west from Pensacola had been stalled due to inclement weather. This eastbound six o'clock would be the last train out of

Jubilee before Tuesday. We apologize for any inconvenience. Thanks for traveling SunTran.

The line forgot it was a line, rushed forward to crash against the pane, which kept the ticket seller safe from us.

I fit myself against the counter when the crowd came to press at my back. The counter cut beneath my ribs. The glass chilled my cheek. The speak-hole pressed its ridges against my ear. If the woman selling tickets had said something to me, anything, I would have heard her clearly.

She said nothing. She retreated into the storeroom and locked the door. I've seen a chained dog back like that into its kennel instead of scrapping, because it knows it is chained, knows if the fight sours it cannot run.

The pressure of the crowd came in waves, rippling forward and subsiding, as if a hand had shoved the ones farthest back. The woman who had been behind me in line pressed against me. My body dented her belly. Her nose brushed the top curve of my right ear. I had rarely been so close to anyone. She breathed too fast, too shallow through that nose. Her breath whistled shrill down my neck. I would have liked to tell her, "Calm down," but my jaw was pressed hard to the Plexiglas. I could not speak. I stood quiet in the wash of her breath.

We pinched Happy Waggoner on her last night. We pinched her in the showers. A clinic down the road had donated a weighing machine to the House. It was digital with an attached height rod. The Matron had taken the donors on a tour of the property, so we showered that night unsupervised. Briony was the first to take Happy's belly in her fingers and twist. Happy laughed.

Happy pushed Briony back into the wall, and the nails tied into Briony's hair clinked.

I don't know who pinched Happy second or third, but there were plenty who didn't like her, plenty ready to join in. I joined in. I knelt over Happy with them, and I remember I looked down once, and I couldn't tell which hands were mine. It didn't matter that Happy had gone quiet beneath our fingers. It's bull what they say, that if you go limp they'll leave you alone. I've seen a cattle dog tear into a possum in the yard. The possum the whole time stayed limp, though it wasn't dead to start. It didn't matter that Happy had stopped laughing. It didn't matter that her lips were thick and full over her teeth, not like any monster. All that mattered was the lifting and tugging of skin, folding her into ridges. It mattered that everyone just for a moment was feeling in their fingers the very same thing. If Happy had been made of clay, we would have left her with ridges like an armadillo's, like a tiled roof. She was not clay, so her skin snapped back when we released it, the way bay waves flatten when the wind dies.

People always want to know about beginnings. Who started it? Why? How? The real question, the interesting question, is how it ends.

We stopped pinching Happy, left her lying there on the gray hospital tile of the showers. We stopped pushing that day in the SunTran station. Gave up. Subsided. Like a riptide cut loose of the moon.

Why didn't we go on trying until we collapsed into each other, the waiting and pressing relieved, the bodies gone into a single body? I wouldn't have minded that. Then we'd only need one ticket, all of us, for the six o'clock train.

One man had sprained his wrist. One girl had bit her tongue not through, but near enough. The rest of us weren't hurt. We expected to be hurt. We checked ourselves for small dents or scratches, to be sure.

A woman called emergency response about the girl's tongue. They would send someone, the dispatch said, but the river was over the sandbag wall in Shreveport. People stood on roofs in Bossier City. They would send someone as soon as they had someone to send.

The ones with tickets hadn't been caught in the press. They sat apart. They said, "I don't know what gets into people," and "I couldn't have taken an hour more in this place." They hid their tickets, slipped them into the center of just-begun books, against the soles of old loafers. Only Sarah May Shell kept hers visible. When she saw me looking at her, she waved her ticket—perhaps in greeting, perhaps to remind me why I was there in the Sun-Tran station and how I could leave.

But when the ticket seller ventured finally from her storeroom, I waved the next woman forward. "It's not so urgent for me," I said, and it was true. The waiting ones bit their nails. They gripped the hands of their children. They couldn't stand it, staying in this place meant for passing through. I didn't mind. I was comfortable here, comfortable in the moment before a ticket was bought, when you could decide to travel either way.

The woman said, "Thanks, doll."

I waved the next man forward, and the one behind him. For fifteen minutes, I stood just beside the ticket window, gesturing with my hand when it was time for the next customer. They thanked me. One asked me if the restroom was open for use. One asked me the number for a Jubilee cab.

Sarah May Shell left on the six o'clock train. She came up to me before. I had by that time become popular. Customers brought me their tickets, so I could point them toward the proper train car. I fit yellow address tags onto luggage to make everything more official.

She told me I should go see Mary in the grotto. "Bring her a flower for her trouble, and she'll set you right."

I didn't bother correcting her again. I reached for her ticket, and she offered it to me just out of kindness. She knew which car was hers. She didn't need my pointing.

I pointed anyway. "Car five," I said.

"Thanks, kid," she said.

When she'd left, I walked through the double doors into the parking lot. There was nobody keeping me in the SunTran station in Jubilee.

I'd told the Matron I pinched Happy Waggoner first, just the way Briony said. All the girls were there when I confessed. All the girls agreed. They knew it wasn't true. I knew. Happy knew. But Happy said, "It was. It was Blue." She said it like she was proud. I wished I'd been the one to quiet Happy under my fingers, the one to surprise her in the showers, to still her laughter. I'd like to be mean and unafraid, the sort of person Happy respected.

Sarah May Shell thought I was like that, driven by a thirst so great I'd kill for it. In truth my thirst was small and indecisive. Often, I'd just lick my lips, and it was gone.

The man who worked the bistro followed me out of the Sun-Tran station. "I don't like that yelling," he said. "I don't like that blood."

"None of us likes it," I said.

He rapped his knuckles on the fender of Sarah's truck. "You're leaking coolant."

I looked at the drips plunking from the fender into the mud. I said, "That's tomato juice." The tomatoes in the heat of the truck must have split their skins.

"You put tomato juice in your radiator?"

"I've been thinking about getting a job here. Flagman. Switchman. Something."

"You don't want to do that," he said. "You don't want to live in Jubilee unless you've been living here all your life."

"I belong here."

He shook his head. "Just because you get kicked out of someplace else doesn't mean you can stay here."

"I'm the one bringing the lilies," I said. "It's me." Not a lie, not exactly. More like a wish. A promise.

"Tomato juice'll gum up your radiator," is all he said.

I rested my weight on the rear bumper, leaned my head against the bed gate as if I owned that truck. I said, "She gets me where I want to go."

But I didn't want to go anywhere. I wanted to stay in Jubilee.

I'd visit Mary in the grotto. I would not prattle at him. I would stand with my feet on top of his feet. I'd brush my lips over his fingers without wrinkle or nail. I'd wedge a lily stalk between his palms, because it was custom, though I know stone can't do a thing with a lily.

THE DARING LIFE
OF PHILIPPA COOK
THE ROGUE

—◆—

Wherein is treated how they came to be a Rogue, and by being so what happened to them.

Deposition taken before John Pott, Esquire, Governor, James Town, on this 2nd day of April, 1629

I am Philippa Cook, and yes, I know something of devils. I am twenty years old, or thereabout. I am both a man and a woman, as I said already to the Captain Clayborne when he did ask, and as the three ladies sitting among you in the court might also attest, having after some bickering and contention amongst themselves come to a consensus of my sex based on three independent inspections.

The court charges that I, on the Feast of St. Nicholas in the house of Captain John Clayborne, did lie with the maid of John Clayborne, the woman known as Great Bessie. As I, before and during this unfortunate lay, was attired as a man, the court proposes to charge me, as a man, with lewd misconduct before the jury, an unmarried servant being unfit to lie with any woman.

I do not contest the charge that I, on the Feast of St. Nicholas in the house of Captain John Clayborne, lay with his maid, a woman named Bethany. I have loved in my life both women and men, and I have known the Goodwoman Bethany. However, I fail to acknowledge the court's ability to try me as a man simply because I was clothed as one. I currently live so attired, because the Claybornes hired me as a man to work their tobacco fields. I still venture out on occasion in women's garb to get a bit for my catt.

After this testimony, the court ordered that it shall be published in the plantation where Cook liveth that he is a man and a woman, that all the inhabitants may take note thereof, and that he shall go clothed in man's apparel, only his head in a woman's coyfe and crofcloth with an apron before him, and that he shall give sureties to the court of his good behavior from quarter court to quarter court until the court release him.

From: Shoo Caddick [shooflyshoo@gmail.com]
To: Mo Silver [nomo4u@hotmail.com]
Fri 12/5/2018 7:46:42 PM

I received the scans of Philippa Cook's letters and can't wait to read them. To think they've been in the Netherlands all this time. Yesterday, I booked passage to Amsterdam on a cargo ship. I'd like to see the original letters in person and, if we can agree on a fair price, purchase them. I've wanted to visit Amsterdam for years now. I've heard it's a great place to be queer.

A bit about me: I'm an actor, not a historian, by training. I came across Philippa's story while playing the servant in a manor home in historic Jamestown. Philippa fascinates me. My girl-friend, Reed, says I'm possessed by them, and I do think of myself sometimes as a sort of reincarnation. I'm not connected to them like you are, not an actual descendant, but I left home at sixteen, like Philippa did. I've worked half a dozen odd jobs, and I've left every one of them. Like Philippa I understand it's impossible to make a life in Virginia. Philippa left Virginia and never looked back. That's my plan, too.

I booked passage without asking Reed. I don't think you need to ask your girlfriend every time you decide to cross the Atlantic. Reed, apparently, does. When I told her you had two letters writ-ten by Philippa, and I was going to Amsterdam to get them, she said, Did you consider me while making this plan? I had. I'd con-sidered her, and I'd considered the timing was shitty. Reed de-fends her thesis next month. Still, I thought she'd be excited. Philippa brought us together, once. Reed liked to remind me they were a colonist and had probably raided the Mattaponi and the Pamunkey. I liked to remind Reed they were indentured, so if they'd raided anybody, it was only because they'd been ordered to. Reed liked to remind me that didn't absolve them. We agreed on one thing—we both loved a Rogue.

Your letters didn't interest Reed. Most likely forgeries, she said, which is just like an academic, so skeptical. I don't under-stand why you want to be like Philippa, she said. Their life was a tragedy.

Tragedy. That's a big word. You don't see me going around saying whose life is or isn't a tragedy.

You need Philippa, Reed said to me. You need to believe you're from somewhere. She'd said that before. She'd said that a hundred times, and I think we were both a little surprised to find ourselves, at the end of her saying it, uncoupled, facing each other across the threshold of her apartment. Me in the hall outside. Her with her hand on the door, closing the door, which was her right. She paid for that door. It was her right to close it and leave me to figure out my own shit in the cold.

Before she shut that door, Reed said, I knew you'd take off. Like Philippa did. Like a man. Like the worst sort of man. I should have argued with her, but I didn't, because when she said, Like Philippa, I felt a surge of pride.

I should arrive in Amsterdam on December 20, assuming no delays. Hold the letters for me, would you?

**From Governor John Pott, James Town,
to Peter Minnewit, Director, Dutch West India Company,
on this 8th of May 1629**

Please be aware of the probable arrival of a servant of this colony by the name of Phillip Cook, who was judged by the quarter court of James Town to be guilty of misconduct with a maidservant, which did result in a child, and so sentenced to a probation with regular presentations at the quarter court. He has disregarded the presentations, the contract of his indenture, and the responsibility of his fatherhood, fleeing across the Chesapeack. We believe he intends to evade the law by taking up residence in your colony.

Given his departure, it was thought fit by the general assembly here in James Town—the Governor himself giving sentence in Cook's absence—that Cook should be branded a Rogue and stand four days with his ears nailed to the pillory, and I do ask that you make haste to return him that he might stand this penalty.

I warn you also that this person Cook does wield his sex and clothes as another man wields a sword, striking with first one blade then the other, as is most convenient for him. Though I've not had the opportunity of inspecting him myself, I've heard from sources I trust not only that his sex is aberrant, but that at knee, where the leg joins the thigh, he hosts a pair of lidless eyes, and his feet are like the talons of a bird, which is the reason he avoids the bath.

I trust you will undeceive him of the notion that your colony offers respite for the criminals of James Town and send him back at once.

**Jan Braeman, Secretary of Isaack de Rasieres,
Provincial Secretary, dwelling upon the Heerengracht,
not far from the West India House, to Governor John Pott,
James Town, 18 June 1629**

Philippa Cook did arrive in this colony not three days after your letter. I appreciated the forewarning, as it saved us much confusion. Soon after she arrived, she presented herself at the church. She looked not unwell but weary from her travels, which she'd made without ample food or companionship. She denies the crime of which you accuse her, and she denies fathering any child—this latter point comes as no surprise, as she is such the woman in face and dress.

I fear the days of the Director and members of his Council are much taken up with the managing of this colony. It's been left to me, then, to translate your letter and determine how best to handle this matter. I hope you'll give me leave here to unburden myself of a sorrowful circumstance. It pleased the Lord, seven weeks after we arrived in this country, to take from me my good partner, who had been to me, for more than sixteen years, a virtuous, faithful, and altogether amiable yoke-fellow; and I now find myself alone with three children, very much discommoded, without her society and assistance.

I must see, then, this Philippa's arrival as a blessing of the Lord. I have two small daughters, and there are no maidservants here to be had, which makes Philippa's service invaluable and greatly decreases any concern she'd take up with one. She's a fine seamstress and a good nurse to the children. They especially enjoy her tales of the Battle of Rhé, which she recounts with the blunt and bluster of a seasoned army man. She has determined to start a garden come spring and is planning the rows and the vegetables, which she calls by the queerest names: Sea Flower and Muske Melon. It's a quiet life for her here, which helps an excitable woman.

Whatever her guilt, I cannot recommend that she be returned, nor can I ensure that if you send men into this colony after her they will be welcomed. We at the Manhattoes have no men to escort back to James Town those pitiable servants which slip through the fingers of the English.

From: Shoo Caddick [shooflyshoo@gmail.com]
To: Mo Silver [nomo4u@hotmail.com]
Fri 12/13/2018 2:24:07 AM

I hope my last email didn't put you off, as my writing was fueled not only by my excitement but also by a box of cheap wine.

Philippa's letters aren't what I expected. Not bad, just unfamiliar. It's like the sag I feel after I have sex with someone for the first time and realize we're not perfectly matched, not two halves of the same whole.

It hasn't changed my plans to come to the Netherlands, though my ship's delayed. Stuck in its port of departure. It might arrive three days or ten days from now. When I told Reed about the delay, she said I might have flown for twice the money and a tenth the time, which I think she could have kept to herself. I asked if I could stay with her until the ship came. She said she didn't think that would be healthy. Unhealthy. Like I was the grease soaking into her gluten-free pizza. So I'm crashing with my friend Nina.

It didn't take as long as I expected to undo my life. In a few hours, I'd pawned my things worth pawning and packed the rest into a duffel I carry slung over my shoulder. With the rest of my time, before the ship arrives, I'll busk as Philippa outside historic Jamestown, where Reed volunteers on the weekends. I've made myself a bonnet from a linen napkin. It was easier to make than I expected, almost like someone else was moving my hands. Like Philippa was moving them. Then Philippa moved them right over this dress of Nina's, the front panel of which has become my apron. If Nina misses it, there'll be the devil to pay. That's what Philippa would say.

Philippa Cook to Rupert Cook, 7th October 1629, Newcastle-Upon-Tyne, Westgate, third house on the left, use the side door, watch the top step, give my mother a kiss from me.

Brother, I write to you from the colonies to describe the circumstances of my departure from my indenture, about which perhaps you have heard. This is the truth of it, whatever other tales you might encounter. I have seen the devil, brother. The devil is a babe.

When Bethany came with it in a sack, I thought it was currants. She said it's a baby. I thought it must have come stillborn, which would have been a blessing, given it's not cheap to bring up a child in the colonies. She, being indentured, would remain indentured all her life for that child, then the child indentured also. Then I saw it move. It thrust one arm against the cloth.

I asked to see it, which she allowed. There was nothing of me in the face or in the sex. Satisfying myself on that account, I handed it back to her. She said she wanted me to sew something for it to be baptized. Doesn't have to be big, she said. I could have sewed her a swaddle from two handkerchiefs, that's how big it was. I agreed.

I asked her was it Clayborne's babe. She said I had no business asking questions like that, which I contested given the nature of our relationship. It's a devil, she said. I said it wasn't, but now I think she had the right of it. Devilish, it was. Maybe it's yours, she said, as if teasing me, but I heard the trick behind her teasing, and I said it couldn't be. She said it had to be somebody's, considering the natural laws of these things and the cost of a child, which she couldn't bear alone. Somebody has to help me with it, she said, looking at me. I couldn't do that. I couldn't help her, and I said that. I wouldn't allow her to put on me half the burden of this babe, tether me to the child and to this cursed place and to my indenture for all of this life and into the next one.

I offered her another solution. I know how it's done. You can use a rock or you can use a pillow or you can swing it against a post. No need for Clayborne nor any person of the house to know. She looked at me like I was suggesting an impossible thing. Do you remember the uniformed devils at Rhé, who knew the ladders were too short for the castle walls, but ordered us boys up them anyway? Do you remember how we set them up against the wall, and the boys went up one after another, climbing climbing like they didn't know they'd end at a face of white stone? Her face was like theirs when I suggested ridding her of the babe. Like I was calling upon her to climb and climb, knowing it would lead nowhere.

She said she'd bring the babe to Clayborne if I refused to help her. I said she should do as she wanted, as it was not my affair. I should have known by then the game she meant to play. She went before Clayborne with the child, and she told him it was mine. He agreed with her. He had reason enough to agree. He's married with four sturdy children still in England. Clayborne is a man like a bull who once locked and charging must charge on until his horns meet some wood or flesh, and he locked those horns on me. He insisted the babe was mine, insisted I go before the quarter court to answer for it. The court made me a fool in all but name, so I left.

The morning I left, I went to Bethany's room, but the child was there beside her, its eyes open and watching me, old old eyes, no babe's eyes those. I knew the way you know a thing in your bones if I took a step closer it would wail for Clayborne, call him down on me and watch with no pity as he swung the bully club into the backs of my knees. Bethany was peaceful, sleeping. Loath was I to disturb her. Loath was I to stay.

Do not worry the family about me. They are kind enough here. Still, I'd give any limb to be home with you. If you have the coin, buy return passage on the next ship bound for the colonies and send word to me. I'll await her at port.

Give my love to mother, to father, to sister &c.

From: Shoo Caddick [shooflyshoo@gmail.com]
To: Mo Silver [nomo4u@hotmail.com]
Wed 12/17/2018 11:45:14 AM

Are you receiving my emails? Let me know as soon as possible, immediately if possible. My ship has come. We shove off in an hour's time, and I can't afford to pay for internet on board.

I've made enough, busking, to buy the letters at the posted price. Raising that money took some doing. At the start, I kept to Philippa's script. I recited the court transcript and the letters, which I've memorized. I improvised only when a boy tried to join me on my milk crate or a man tried to strip me of my apron. But the people walked right past me, turned their backs on me any-time a carriage rolled by, so I elaborated. I hiked up my apron and jigged. I peppered in jokes from Philippa's time, like the one about the captain who had his arm shot off and, as the wound was being dressed, started laughing. When asked what was the matter, he said, I've always wanted my penis to be longer than my arm, and now it is. Then, I had a crowd. Then, the bills dropped into my bonnet. One man left a hundred-dollar bill clipped to a note that said, *Nice show, kid. Buy a corset.*

Yesterday, Reed came past right as I told that joke to a crowd off a Philly tour bus. Reed stopped in front of my miniature audience. Reed had once loved my jokes, had once laughed so hard she pulled a muscle. Now, she was serious, disapproving. She said, loudly, What are you doing, Shoo? The bus crowd, sensing a domestic altercation, fled without dropping so much as a dime into my bonnet.

I stood there in front of Reed, a little out of breath from the routine. You ruined the show, I said.

She said, You look ridiculous. I did, I'm sure. The Jamestown court ridiculed Philippa. That was the point. Still, just like that she punctured that warm feeling I had, that puffed-up feeling of performing for an audience that's on your side, that feeling you could make them laugh or scream with a word, with a twitch of your shoulder. You look like a boy, Reed said. Reed doesn't like boys. What are they good for? she's asked me more than once. Why do we need them?

I am a boy, I said, which was one of my Philippa lines.

Philippa never dressed that way, Reed said. Philippa left Jamestown so they wouldn't have to dress that way.

What's your point? I said.

Are you making fun of them?

I'm making money. I'm trying to get to Amsterdam. I pointed roughly east, to emphasize this. Reed knocked my hand away, and right there something glinted. She had started something, touching me that way, roughly.

She said, There are other ways to make money.

Are those my earrings? I said, pointing to her ears, and they were. A pair of silver hoops.

Reed's hand went to one earring. No, she said.

I said, Bullshit, and a woman walking by paused to ask Reed if she was all right, like I was bothering her. Maybe I was. Bothering her. The earrings were mine, even if Reed wouldn't cop to it. She stood there, the nerve of her, with her research grant and her downtown apartment and everything a person could want, refusing me a pair of plated silver hoops. I felt not anger but a ruthless sense of injustice. I walked right up to her, and she froze, startled. You're scaring me, she said. This made me sad, but not sad enough to stop me reaching out when I got close and taking the earrings, quick but gentle, from her ears. She caught my wrist, and we hovered there for a moment, wondering would she twist my wrist, would I pull back, would we hurt each other? We didn't. She let go.

People think it's brave, Reed said, picking up and leaving. It's not brave. It's the easiest thing to run away like that.

I hadn't found it easy—the delays, no place to stay. I hadn't found it easy at all, I said. I couldn't live all my life in Richmond, Virginia, and I said that, too.

It's a fine place to live, Reed said. That's the problem with Reed, the real maddening thing about Reed—she's content. She said, We're not living in 1629.

You're not, I said.

You're not, either.

I told her my ship was waiting for me, though it wasn't my ship and it wasn't waiting for me but for a load of cereal grain coming by train from Iowa. Still, I loved the sound of it. My ship. I could see it—the waiting ship, which in my mind was wooden and rigged for sailing. I walked away.

They're laughing at you, Reed called after me. Don't you see that?

That's the point.

You're humiliating yourself, she said. She sounded so satisfied, like naming what I was doing solved something. Shoo, she called. I didn't turn. You don't have to answer when a person calls you, not even if they call you by name. Philippa taught me that.

I rode the train back to Richmond. There was one baby on the train, and I tried to flirt with the baby. I made little faces, puckered my lips, wrinkled my nose. Usually, babies like me. I made a whir I thought it would like, a noise like a fire alarm. It started to cry, at which point the man holding it gave me a look like I'd ruined something that wasn't mine to begin with.

Let me know when you get this email. I don't need any lengthy reply, just a note that you've still got the letters, that you'll be there when I arrive.

Mrs. Hendrina Demkis, New York, to Mr. Edward Gant, College of William and Mary, 22nd April 1710

Yes, I am the Miss Demkis that Minerva Clayborne remembers visiting her estate in fall of 1665. I was just fourteen. I was there with my nursemaid, Philippa Cook. It's astounding Mrs. Clayborne has any memory of that day at all, though I suppose it's true that as the lanterns darken yesterday, they brighten yesteryear. I'll share what I remember to help with your history, though I hardly see how Philippa Cook could feature in a history of Jamestonian indenture. Our servants are paid for their work, their every comfort seen to. I can't say the same of our neighbors to the south.

Jan Braeman was my great-grandfather. He was never a friend of the Claybornes, not that I knew. We'd actually gone that day to visit the home of an esquire, John Pott. Papa Braeman had some need to see him and some business at the courthouse as well.

Papa Braeman always kept characters in his employ, found them at the courthouse or the church house or on the run from an indenturor. A better Calvinist you never saw, but he got airs, Papa Braeman, funny ideas, and when he got them there was nothing to do but go along. For instance, he was in the habit, when he wanted a diversion, of taking his employees out about the town or to prayer meetings, showing them off. That's the reason I ended up traveling with Nurse Philippa down to Newtowne, Virginia.

When I knew Philippa, she was well advanced in years, and it was difficult to get her to focus on a conversation or a sewing job long enough to finish it, but I have it from my grandmother she made the finest bone lace in all New York, and if the samples she showed are any proof, it's true.

My grandmother was brought up by Philippa, her mother dying not long after she arrived in the colonies, and her father busy at the council or at his books. She remembered Philippa as something of a fool, a jester, despite being always dour of countenance. Philippa had a habit of tossing her apron over her shoulder when she walked a distance, which gave her a man's manner and caused my grandmother no end of embarrassment. She set a strange example for the Braeman girls. My grandmother had to learn the hard way not to bunch and tie her petticoat when crossing a muddy road. Philippa thought nothing of things like that.

Philippa had the attic room, from which she would climb sometimes out onto the eaves. Aside from this perch, she rarely left the house. The ones in town did tease her mercilessly and I, knowing some of them from church or school, heard tales of her you wouldn't believe—that she was on the run from the law in Virginia, that she killed babies and ate them, that beneath her coiffe her skull was broken in three places, and so she wore the coiffe always tied very tightly to keep her brain from spilling, that where a person should have feet, she had the claws of a bird. This last one I believed for a time, given the way she perched on our roof and the size of her shoes. To satisfy my curiosity I convinced her once to let me wash her feet in a salt bath, and though they were wide as a man's and misshapen with corns, such that her boots had to be three sizes too large, they were human feet.

Philippa herself told stories scarcely more credible—that she fought against the French on the Isle of Rhé and had gotten a silver medal, as did every man who survived the fight, that her brother went up the ladders to breach the wall, but the ladders were too short for the wall. All around her, she said, boys shouted to pull back the ladders, and the boys on the ladders tried to get down off them, leaping from the tops of the ladders to their death. She says her brother alone made it over the wall. She saw him make it. There was a great lot of smoke from the cannon fire, and when it cleared he'd disappeared into the castle of Rhé or into the sky.

I told her that can't have been, because only boys went to war, and she said, "Well, I was a boy," which made me laugh. Sometimes I think she wanted to make us laugh. Other times she frightened me. If I'd been her child, she said, she'd have dashed my brains out against a rock. When I was little, she threatened to do so anytime I misbehaved, and this terrified me. When I was older, I told her it was a horrid thing to say.

The visit Mrs. Clayborne remembers began when Papa Braeman promised Philippa a trip home to Virginia. She didn't want to go. The whole day before, she was a flurry of nerves. She told Papa Braeman the Claybornes would expect her in men's clothes. She'd been ordered to dress so, she said, by the Jamestown court. I told her that must have been ages ago and surely didn't matter now, but she insisted. She said she didn't want to chance it. Papa Braeman didn't question it. He let her clothe herself from his own wardrobe, which I resented. I'd asked a dozen times to play that way and always been refused.

When we got out to the Pott estate, the Master Pott said his father wasn't able to speak with us, that he'd taken sick. It greatly disappointed Papa Braeman, I can tell you. I think he'd been quite looking forward to reuniting Philippa and Esquire Pott. From what he said they knew each other many years ago. Philippa, I think, was relieved.

But here's the part that will interest you. Later, Papa Braeman had business to attend to, so he left us—Philippa and me—at the old tobacco farm where she had worked, the Clayborne estate. "I worked in the fields," Philippa said, which I suppose was another fib. The Claybornes would not let us inside. They said they had a child sleeping and asked if we could come another time. I said we'd walk the grounds, which we did. Philippa leaned rather hard on my arm, unused at her age to walking a great distance. We went out a little ways, but she tired quickly, so we turned back to the house.

We found on the back porch a servant woman, with whom we passed the remaining time until my great-grandfather came to pick us up. Her name, she said, was Becca, but Philippa insisted on calling her Bethany, which was enough in itself to make me blush. Then what's worse, Philippa started speaking to her as if they were the best of friends, saying, "Bethany it's been such a long while since I've seen you, and so many things have happened in my life." She went on, listing them. She said, "Do you remember the blouse I sewed for you?" The woman was no older than I and couldn't have known the first thing about Philippa. She said she didn't remember and was sorry. She said she never knew anyone named Bethany. She was perfectly polite, but you could see she had work to be doing, and Philippa was keeping her from it. Then Philippa asked her what she was going to do when she was finished with the Claybornes, and I blushed red as beetroot, but Becca only said she'd be singing with the angels then. She said she'd better get tea set on the table and escaped into the house.

When I apologized to Philippa that Becca hadn't remembered, Philippa said, "Well, I remember. I remember all of it." Then Philippa took a small, well-crafted sack from a hook on the house wall. She folded it carefully and slipped it down the front of her pants. I told her she'd get us in trouble, stealing like that. She shook her head. "It's not stealing. I made it."

"It's not yours," I told her. I thought of all the bone lace, all the dresses she'd sewn for us over the years, wondering if she thought herself the owner of every one. "It's stealing all the same."

"They were never nice," Philippa said, and in her face something surfaced bright and vindictive and terrible cruel, so that I thought she would have taken more than the cloth if there'd been more left out for the taking. I thought the Claybornes were right to keep us on the porch, to fear her. But a second passed, and the look was gone.

I wish you the best with your history. The Clayborne place was lovely enough to my eyes. Philippa, I'm afraid, was none too fond of Newtowne as it is now. Too built up for her, too populated.

It must be a quality of age, and I'm sure my grandchildren

will say the same of me, but Philippa had a number of peculiar ideas. She once told me of a man shot in the thigh, who complained of unbearable pain. When they looked to see what was the matter—beyond his being shot—they found the bud-leaf of a Sea Stocke Gillowflower poking its green head up from his wound. They removed it, taking enough flesh they would not bare the roots, because the Gillowflower is a rare plant. They bound him up again and carried both man and plant home on the *Rochel*, where on arrival the one was buried in the potter's field, the other in the Lord's Garden at Canterbury.

I told her that can't have happened. It was a nightmare, probably.

"We put them in the ground, and we left them there," she said. "Not a nightmare, no, it's just something I remember."

From: Reed Turner [rturner@virginia.edu]
To: Shoo Caddick [shooflyshoo@gmail.com]
Wed 12/17/2018 6:23:04 PM

I don't think we should talk anymore.

I shouldn't write any more than that, but here I am, hoping this reaches you before you reach the Netherlands.

First, every historian with an interest in Philippa Cook agrees they were intersex and incapable of having children. Second, only one in thirty indentured servants could read; fewer still could write. Philippa Cook left behind no letters and no descendants. You're crossing the ocean for a fake, Shoo. You have to know that.

Shoo Caddick, SS *Argus*, Atlantic Ocean, to Mo Silver, Amsterdam, on this 31st December 2018

20 December

Reed and I are kaput. I'm sad, but I can't say I'm devastated. I anticipate my recovery has been aided in large part by the air here, by that line where the sea meets the sky, which blurs in the early mornings; even by the smell of the ship, which is by no means pleasant, and the roar of the propellers on the A deck, which keeps me up at night.

It's a quiet life. I'm writing this by hand. Yesterday, I tried to spot a group of islands, but there were clouds. Today, I pocketed six biscuits in the mess hall and scattered the crumbs on the A deck for gulls. Even out here there are gulls. We take our meals on rubber place mats, in case the ship rolls while we eat. Yesterday, it was stew. Today, it was southwest chicken. Yesterday, the ship rolled fore to aft. Today, it's rolling side to side. I'm nearly through the antacids I brought, which I expected to last the trip.

31 December

We pull into the harbor today.

I know you might not be there at all. You might have traveled to London for work. You might have moved. You might have had a sudden death in the family. You might not be of Philippa's lineage. You might have sold the letters. They might have been penned by another Philippa Cook altogether. I might have left Virginia, have left Reed, all for nothing. I lay awake last night, bedeviled by these concerns.

I comforted myself with this thought: Philippa Cook lived a

daring life, and I must be at least as daring. And here is another thing Philippa would understand. This morning, standing on the top deck in a light drizzle, watching the rain and wave spray darken the metal of the cereal containers, I was filled with a peace that lasted hours, hours before I could muster any sense of fear at all.

Philippa Cook to Rupert Cook, 2nd April 1630, Newcastle-Upon-Tyne, Westgate

Brother, I have had no reply to my last letter to you. I think they didn't send it. I've given this one to the eldest girl in the house, who has promised to post it for me. I trust her more than her father, but I can't trust her entirely, of course.

Yesterday, I was sitting on the eaves just outside my window. I often sit there, looking out over the harbor. I thought I saw you. I saw a boy who looked just like you, and for a moment I thought it was your specter. There's plague, I've been told, in Newcastle, and I wondered if you had taken ill and had come to visit me before trundling on to the stony vaults of Paradise. I called to you, brother, thinking you might rise up beside me, the pull of the Earth no obstacle for a haunt. Instead, the boy turned his face to me and went very still, and I recognized the eldest Braeman girl, dressed like a lad, headed off into town.

I went after her, of course, dragged her home by her collar and paddled her. The nerve of the girl. If her father had seen, I'd be cast out for certain. He'd think it my example. The girl's face after her punishment, streaked with mucus and wailing, was the face of a babe, and for a moment I thought of Bethany's babe, of the life I'd fled. I never escaped it, is what I thought. I will die in this house a servant and a woman, a woman for all the rest of my days. A terrific thought, but I know the terror will pass, as terror does, into something sweeter, almost a comfort.

I write to relieve you of any responsibility you may feel to find return passage for me. These days the salt burns my nose, and the wet aches my bones, and my stomach is none too fond of the upset of the sea. I'll remain here, always your sibling and your friend, Philippa.

BUMP

—

To those who accuse me of immoderate desire, I say look at the oil executives. Look at the gold rush. Look at all the women who want a ring and romance and lifelong commitment, and then look again at me. Me, I just want a person to dance the two-step with on Friday nights, a person who won't mind if I wear a shirt with maroon sequins or, occasionally, a strap-on pregnancy bump. In return, I offer a woman who can get by on little. I keep myself spotless. My car and my nails and my résumé, I polish. I polish myself. I polish myself until I shine.

The first thing that drew me to Len was that anyone could tell this was a man who had worked to be where he was and would work to stay there. Born on a cattle ranch an hour outside Gainesville, he'd made partner at an Atlanta law firm, the firm that once represented Coca-Cola against the state. He wore a suit and tie to work even on casual Fridays. He had no southern accent. On our first date, I asked him about the accent. He said, "I did away with it." Like it was nothing, doing away with a whole part of yourself. When I talk about polish, this is what I mean.

Representing Coca-Cola is reprehensible, of course, and I've told him that, but still I admire his dedication.

When I told him, on our third date, I was trans, he said, "That makes no difference." Another reason I love him. Not like my Nana, who had a conniption, said I was risking my job and my health and her livelihood in the bargain, since she lived with me and counted on me to provide for her. And I did lose that first job. I made mistakes. I worked a miserable job for six years just for the health insurance. But a year ago I got a new part-time job, a better job, and here I am.

Len didn't care I was trans. Now, I think maybe I should have asked for more than ambivalence, but for three years I was happy with Len. Friday evenings, we danced the two-step at Dig Down, and he maneuvered me expertly through the crowd. He never trod on my foot. Not once. Weekends, he came over and cooked pasta. Sometimes, when he was feeling ambitious, he cooked crepes. He was devoted to me. His crepes were terrible.

His wife, Melinda, sometimes invited me to the nail salon or for sushi. I was grateful to her for the invitations, though I always declined. We were cordial, Melinda and I. We understood how to fit together, how to help each other. We both believed it was a good thing, even a relieving thing, to divide up the responsibility of caring for a man.

With Len, for the first time in my life, I could honestly say, "I am content."

This all ended, of course. I can trace the descent to one moment four months ago when I was eating lunch with my coworker Julie, and she asked me how I was feeling at the end of my first

trimester. Now, I had most certainly, most definitely not mentioned any baby or being pregnant or even wanting to be pregnant, which is something I continue to want quietly, since it is
impossible, and there is something inherently shameful in wanting, concretely—not a whim, not a wish, but a cold hard desire—
after an impossible thing. Uterine transplants are at least six
years down the road. By then I'll be past childbearing age. I know
this, and I accept it, but there Julie was acting as if I was carrying
a baby, and there I was, to my great surprise, going along with it.

I should have said I wasn't pregnant, whatever she'd heard,
whatever rumor had been weaving itself together in the break
room, but she smiled at me like we were sharing a new secret. She
had been through two pregnancies, the second more difficult
than the first. Everyone in the office knew the details. Her smile
invited me to put my swollen feet up on conference tables, to send
my ultrasounds to the ALL office email. Right down into my
abdomen, that smile warmed me. She thought I was pregnant,
and so it seemed possible, and I smiled and said, "I feel better
than ever," and that's how I'm in the mess I'm in now.

Desire has its own rhythms. It overwhelms and subsides. At the
height of my contentment with Len, I'd nearly forgotten how it felt
to want something—the pull and the thrill of it. Then two years
into our relationship, Len said to me, "We're pregnant." For a
single, startled moment I'd thought he meant the two of us, but he
was talking of course about his wife, Melinda, about the baby we
hadn't met yet, who would be born to that happy couple five

months later on the winter solstice, a solstice baby, born on a night of astronomical importance with toe-thumbs and a full head of hair. I called that baby the aphid. I cared for the aphid on Saturdays to give Melinda a break, and I enjoyed my relationship with them, which was something like a cousin or an aunt. Melinda was a deliberate mother. She published articles on her blog about cloth diapers and raising children in nontraditional family structures. She didn't let just anyone watch the aphid, but she let me.

Maybe it was my time with the aphid that got my coworkers talking. Maybe they sensed some baby pheromone. Or possibly the rumor started when I complained to another coworker that I'd been nauseated in the mornings. I'd put the nausea down to a new progesterone or to a habit of breaking my fast with Lemoncocco seltzer, but she said, "Are you pregnant?"

"What do you think?" I said. That was a real question. Did I seem pregnant? I wanted to know. But she just pressed her lips together into a private, secret smile and waltzed away.

After Julie asked about my first trimester, I started thinking about children. Night and day, for three nights and four days, I thought about them. Finally, one morning I texted Len, *Would you want to have a child with me?*

Good morning to you

I texted, *Not immediately, but one day.*

Two families is a lot

I'm just asking if you'd want to.

When we met up that evening, I asked him again.

"The logistics would be difficult," he said.

"So you don't want to."

"I didn't say that. I said the logistics would be difficult. We'd have to adopt."

"We wouldn't have to adopt," I said, though I couldn't name an alternative to adoption.

"I don't think this is a conversation we need to have tonight," he said. "I think this is a conversation we should have in a year, in a few years."

I said nothing, impressed into silence by his vision of longevity. I don't know anyone but Len who anticipates conversations they'll have in a few years.

People think contentment is a gentle, warm thing, like bathwater, that needs only occasional replenishing to keep it from turning slowly tepid. In my experience, contentment often requires more ruthless and more immediate defending. After leaving Len that evening, I defended. I went through Facebook and unfriended the yoga instructor who posted a photo of herself nursing her two-year-old while in forearm stand. I unfriended the librarian who posted a photo in which she read Tolstoy while pumping, tagged it #myruminantlife. I wrote a long post on Facebook about the insensitivity of self-congratulatory motherhood. I included references to half a dozen recent articles, like "The Peak of Selflessness: Motherhood."

Afterward, I felt better. It wasn't until Len called that I realized the article about selflessness had been written by his wife.

"She's not upset. She just doesn't understand. She thought you were getting along," he said.

"We are getting along. It's a difference of opinion, that's all. It's not personal."

"Well, it feels personal to her."

"Melinda could decide at any moment, at the drop of a hat, that she doesn't want me spending time with the aphid, and I could do nothing. How do you think that feels for me?"

"Don't call him the aphid."

"Don't gender them."

"Melinda has asked you not to call our baby the aphid."

"At any moment, she could decide she doesn't want me around."

"She'd never decide that."

"But she could."

"She likes you," he said. Len often told me someone liked me. It was reflexive for him, a way to smooth any ruffles, avoid an argument. "She thinks you're great," he said.

"I think she's great," I said, which seemed beside the point. "I just need distance." This wasn't something I'd planned to say, but in the moment it seemed necessary, a way to save face.

He was quiet. I'd surprised him. "We thought you liked spending time with Aster."

We. A word I hated. A word that declared to the listener, You Are Not One of Us.

"Melinda's trying. Sometimes I think you don't appreciate how hard she's trying. She wants you to feel welcome. She wants you to feel like part of the family."

"I'm not part of your family."

"Louie, you knew what this was when we started dating. If it's not what you want—"

"It is what I want," I said. It wasn't everything I wanted, but I'd long since stopped imagining that any single person could satisfy want in another.

"We can take some time away. Like you said. We can check in next week."

I could feel the whole thing getting away from me. "Aren't I watching Aster this Saturday?"

"Do something for yourself on Saturday."

"So I'm not allowed at your house now on Saturdays?"

"I can't keep up with you, Louie. Two minutes ago, you said you want distance. I say let's try distance, and you're angry."

"I want a family." I waited for him to respond.

"That's not on the table, Louie. For us, for now, that's not on the table."

So. There it was.

"Let's take some time. Let's check in next week," he said.

I said, "Two weeks," and he raised me to three, and I raised him, and he raised me, and suddenly we were saying good night, and I was wiping the moisture from the screen of my phone and going to get Nana ready for bed, unsure if I'd see him again.

It's not easy, polishing yourself. It's not easy teaching yourself to code or making do with cornstarch as a setting powder or going into debt for a tracheal shave. But there's comfort in knowing you can do it, in relying only on yourself. I sat down the next Saturday, when I should have been watching the aphid, and searched online for pregnancy bumps. The bumps come in a range of prices and sizes. Every one, according to the reviews, causes the kind of back pain you need a professional to relieve.

Moonbump makes you a custom bump, matching your skin color, your overall dimensions, the stage of pregnancy you're hoping to simulate, and the number—a single, twins, or the triplet bump—all for the price of a used car. If I could afford a Moonbump, I'd have gotten a Moonbump. Instead, I went with the Pregnant Belly by Spirit, which shipped from South Korea and came complete with shoulder straps and an adjustable back belt. I ordered one for four to six months and one for seven to nine months. I chose express shipping. The Pregnant Belly by Spirit got good reviews for the price, though I've since considered whether I should have spent a bit more, invested in a more durable bump.

When my bumps came, I modeled them for Nana. They were cold and slick against my skin, like plastic wrap. I could already feel the weight and tug of the belt, a squeeze that would escalate over hours to a backache.

"That shape says you're having a girl," Nana said into her sausage-and-carrot stew, and I was pleased in spite of myself, cupping the bump, rubbing circles into it, doting on it like people do.

"You going to be in a play?"

"People at work think I'm pregnant." I dabbed her lips with a cloth napkin, which came away pink from the lipstick she wears daily, even on days she doesn't leave her bed.

"And you haven't told them otherwise?"

"I'll correct them. Eventually, I will."

"Pregnancy isn't like hepatitis. You can't clear it up so easy. It ends in a baby."

"I could borrow a baby if I needed one," I said, thinking about the aphid.

"People will find out, Louie. You'll embarrass yourself."

"Len and I have been talking about adoption," I said, which was technically true. We did talk about it, though at this point we weren't even talking that much. We sent sporadic texts—new restaurants worth trying, the tragic dissolution of the Atlanta Silverbacks. Neither of us had suggested meeting up. Perhaps he was waiting for me. I was waiting for him. I felt a punch of sadness that Len wouldn't see me in the bump.

"Takes longer to adopt a kid than to grow one," Nana said. "If you need an excuse for medical leave, why not hemorrhoids, something nobody's going to ask you about."

"This isn't about leave."

"Then what's it about?"

"It's a misunderstanding, that's all. It got out of hand."

She picked up her bowl and slurped the last of her broth, the grease of it shining on her chin. "Well, you better find a way to get it back in hand, Louie. Pregnancy is a temporary condition."

This is the way we spend our evenings, Nana and I.

I was self-conscious my first day at work in the bump. I worried people would find the bulge at my abdomen too sudden, worried people would somehow sense it was a prosthetic and declare me a fraud. But no one mentioned the bump. In the developers meeting, as we worked our way through a demo I'd helped debug, the head developer stood up and insisted I take the chair with extra back support. Julie nodded to me every time I passed her cube, little knowing nods that felt almost like friendship. She invited me to her Code Like a Mother support group. I declined. I was not a mother-to-be. The bump wasn't about motherhood. My pregnancy was an end in itself, the enactment of a ritual, and I approached it that way, as something real but apart, without the purpose of a usual pregnancy. I had an urge to explain this to everyone, but I didn't. They wouldn't understand.

By the end of month four, my first month with the bump, my backache was chronic, and the bump felt as familiar to me as my own breasts. It looked used, well-loved, the silicone at the top left edge repaired with a patch designed for inflatable pools. Weekly, I cleaned the bump with lukewarm water and baby soap, patted it dry. Beneath the bump, my skin went soft and wrinkly, raw at the edges. Where the silicone rubbed, my skin blistered like feet in heels, blisters I soothed with Nana's ointment. This felt like a painful, necessary process, bringing me closer to the bump, opening my insides to it. I wore the bump all day, and I wore it to bed, sleeping on my side, curled around it. I felt more at ease wearing it, and more myself.

In month five, Julie wanted to throw me a shower. If you knew Julie, this would need no further explanation. She's a great one for celebrations. She buys cheap soccer trophies, scrounges them up from yard sales, and gives them away at staff meetings. Any excuse to fill a Thursday afternoon with cake and reusable bubble letters, Julie seizes on it.

I told her I'd rather not have a shower. She said she understood, but later she emailed me a link to a website with various baby shower themes. In the subject line, she'd written, "Which one?" I didn't respond. An hour later she sent me an Outlook reminder for the week's Code Like a Mother gathering, which promised nonalcoholic schnapps and prenatal-friendly yoga.

That evening, as I bathed Nana, hunched over the bump, over the tub, I said, "It's almost like your great-grandbaby." The bump would have been her great-grandbaby. Nana wanted to meet her great-grandbabies. She was planning to hang on until she could.

In the bathtub, Nana made a derisive sound. She dodged the cup of water I attempted to use to rinse her hair. I held the back of her neck to still her while I rinsed. When she climbed out of the tub, she put her hand on the bump. At first, I thought she just needed a grip to steady herself, but it wasn't a steadying touch. It was a loving one. She was drawn to the bump.

I toweled her head, trying to dissuade the thin strands of her hair from twisting up into a cowlick. "I'd name it after you," I said. "If it was a baby."

She pulled her hand back from the bump. "Don't you start thinking that way."

"If, I said." I knew to be careful. I thought of the bump only as the bump. I understood the risk, the delusion—and worse, the grief—inherent in thinking of it as anything else.

"I wanted another one," Nana said, wincing as I patted down her arms, though I was gentle. "After your father," she said, "I wanted a second one. We tried and tried." She touched the bump again.

"Nothing worked?"

"Back then, there weren't so many options. You could eat almonds. You could time your cycle or lie for hours after sex with your pelvis tilted back and a warm compress on your stomach. I did what I could, and it didn't work, and that was that."

"I'm sorry."

"I'm glad. I'm glad we couldn't try and try and try like people these days, couldn't go broke trying, couldn't give whole years to it."

I felt a familiar skip of uncertainty, wondering if this was a veiled criticism of me. "There's nothing wrong with options," I said.

"I guess I wouldn't know. I'm just a country Cajun." This was a line Nana used regularly, when she wanted to dodge an argument or dodge some responsibility. A line she used to pretend she'd been plucked against her will out of Louisiana, dropped into a city she couldn't possibly be expected to understand. She used it to avoid recycling and regular doctor's appointments and public transportation of any sort. "I'm just a country Cajun" seemed self-effacing but in fact worked as a defense, a statement of withdrawal and superiority, implying that we could never understand each other, because I wasn't a country Cajun. To Nana, I wasn't Cajun at all.

"We could go back to Louisiana," Nana said, her voice sly. "That would be one way to escape this pregnancy charade of yours."

"It's not a charade."

"You could tell everyone you want to bring the baby up around family."

She wanted to go back. She made no secret of this. She wanted to visit the grave of her husband. She wanted her funeral service held at the Rose Church, where she'd gone to Mass all her life. She wanted her remains interred in the mausoleum where her mother had been interred.

She wished she'd never left. She blamed my father for moving away, leaving her alone and unable to prevent the slow disintegration of her house, the black mold that constellated on her walls, the roof that gave way completely during Ivan, leaving the house condemned after the storm and Nana with no choice but to move into a home or into my home in Atlanta. I wasn't moving to Louisiana. If I moved, I was heading to the West Coast, where tech companies have enough trans employees to host their own support groups.

I said to Nana, "I don't want to leave the city." I rubbed ointment on her pressure sores. "I have a whole life here—a job, Len, friends at work, opportunities."

"There's no opportunity that will turn that bump into a baby."

I paused, the ointment tube open in my hands. "What if it were true," I said.

"You're not pregnant. You can't get pregnant, Louie. You know that."

I capped the ointment, took Nana's nightgown from the hook, and slipped it over her head. "I read about a man in Connecticut," I said, "a cis man. He was born with a uterus. It's not like it's never happened."

"You know you can't," she said again.

"But if I could, what a thing."

"You're caught up," Nana said. "Preoccupied with what you want."

"I could be spending my evening in a thousand different ways," I said, "and here I am taking care of you." Nana didn't reply. Nana was preoccupied with what she wanted, too.

After Nana's bath, I did two things. I texted Len, asking if he'd like to meet up, and I logged on to my work email and accepted Julie's invitation to that Thursday's Code Like a Mother meeting. I wanted it to be true, what I said to Nana. I wanted to have people in this city, to feel I could spend my evening with Nana or on a date or holding downward dog in a line of six women who were my friends.

Julie responded immediately with a GIF of a child jumping up and down, punching the air. Len took twelve hours, but then wrote back, *Saturday?*

Julie's Code Like a Mother meetings took place at five in a windowless interior break room, the tables pushed against the walls to make space for yoga mats. The MotherCoders were six cis women in their thirties, each recruited personally by Julie. The woman leading the yoga class had studied for twelve years in an ashram in California, paying for her teacher training by working remotely as a hacker for an American finance company.

I was the only one with a bump and tried not to feel conspicuous on this account. The hacker-yogi referred to me by saying, "those of us who are expecting." At first this annoyed me, but after a few minutes I started to think about the things I was expecting. Being brought on full-time at work. Dating someone who wasn't Len, someone who wasn't married. Living with that person in a house without Nana, after Nana. When the hacker-yogi told us to visualize our intent for the practice, I closed my eyes and tried to really see those things, but the bump rose instead, came up before me like a snow moon on the horizon, huge and luminous, blocking everything else from view.

I opened my eyes to see the real bump in the narrow mirror the yogi had brought so we could monitor our form. I watched myself move in that mirror, and I experienced one of those rare, precious moments in which I felt simply attractive—my clavicles delicate, my eyelashes long. Even my rosacea, which had flared as I sweat, gave me a glow. The bump moved with me, part of me. Not a false thing. A thing that served its own purpose, parallel to pregnancy, not a ghost of it, a different thing altogether.

At the hacker-yogi's instruction, I bent into a languorous forward fold, and it was then that something popped. At my shoulder, a pop. I expected pain, but there was no pain. Just the pop and a sudden looseness at my abdomen—and certainty, a mother's certainty, that it was the bump. Sure enough, I felt the silicone start to peel away from my ribs, my body instinctively sucking in a deep breath, which caused it to peel away more quickly, sudden air sharp and painful against skin that had been so long covered, and the bump tipped forward, protruding oddly against my shirt. I clutched it, pressed it flat, and ran for the single-stall bathroom. I made it, just, and locked the door behind me. At the sink, one shoulder strap tore away completely, and the bump flapped forward, pocketing itself in my shirt—a sad, separate thing.

I took it off. The bump settled into the concavity of the sink. I envied the sink for so easily cupping it. How long did I stand there, considering the shape of my body, bumpless, the two separate shapes? Long enough that Julie was worried.

"Louie," she called, knocking. "Louie, you okay?"

This is the moment I come back to, the moment I'd change. Writing it down like this, I am changing it. It's like I'm walking over to that bathroom door, unlocking it and swinging it open. Julie is looking back and forth between me, bumpless, and the bump—me, the bump. I look at Julie's face.

Sometimes, I see confusion there. Sometimes, Julie watches me as if expecting me to collapse in a jumble of pieces. Sometimes, Julie takes up the bump without a word and helps me knot the broken shoulder strap to my bra, securing the bump, and when we've finished she says, "Next time get a Swiss bump. They're sturdier." Sometimes, Julie starts laughing. She laughs and laughs, and the other MotherCoders come and they laugh, and Julie takes the bump and tosses it up in the air like confetti, and the bump, miraculously light, arcs toward the ceiling and down, then the hacker-yogi volleys it up again, then the other women, playing keep-away with the bump as I run back and forth, trying to grab hold of the bump, because every time they volley it upward I feel the punch of their knuckles right in my abdomen. Sometimes, looking at my abdomen, Julie begins to scream. She screams and screams, her mouth wide open, and I look down to see my shirt soaked with blood. I lift up my shirt, and where the bump was there's a wound, my abdomen skinless and bleeding, as if the bump had been sliced clean away, and I tell Julie to help me, bring me the bump, bring me a needle and thread, I will stitch the bump back to me, but Julie won't come any closer, so I'm left to stem the bleeding with the rough paper towels from the dispenser, which are so cheap and useless I run through the whole roll.

Of course, this didn't happen. I didn't open the door. "I'm okay," I called to Julie.

"Are you sure? Should I phone someone for you?"

I tied the strap of the bump to my bra, a quick clumsy knot, obvious beneath my tight shirt. It didn't need to hold forever, just long enough to thank Julie, get to my car. I exited the bathroom.

Julie immediately pressed me into a hug, which put her up against the bump. I felt it shift, slip a quarter inch against my skin, and I thought surely Julie would notice, even if she wrote it off as a kick, but Julie just said, "You'll be fine, you know."

I repeated those words in the front seat of my car, having waved off Julie's offer to escort me to the parking lot. "You'll be fine," I told the bump, cranking up the air conditioner as high as it would go.

I drove home with one hand on the bump, cradling it against my body. The bump clung to me, but not like a child.

I took Friday off work to tend to the bump. I was no seamstress, but I could patch, I could hem. I could mend the bump. I borrowed what I needed from Nana's sewing kit and retreated upstairs to my room. The mending felt like a private thing—not shameful, but best attended to alone, like applying cream to an abdominal rash. Besides, I wanted to spend the day with the bump, caring for it, just the two of us. The bump wasn't what people thought, and that made it vulnerable. I wanted to keep the injured bump away from even Nana's eyes.

I threaded the size eleven needle and pieced the shoulder strap together with a mattress stitch, the stitch surgeons use to minimize scarring when they piece together skin. I worked steadily, enjoying the task, and I discovered when I finished that I had done well. The bump was whole again, the stitches barely visible.

I was to meet Len Saturday at seven at a no-frills beer and wings joint. The joint was within walking distance of his house and a quick drive from mine. A significant choice, this restaurant. By suggesting it, Len communicated his desire to make the reunion between us a nonevent. I parked on the street and sat, absently rubbing the bump, considering my options.

Impossible. It was impossible that Len didn't know about the bump. Seven o'clock passed. Then seven ten. I got out of the car with the bump, wore it all the way to the door of the restaurant. I saw Len, seated, waiting for me. He hadn't seen me. I stood on the threshold, but I couldn't enter the restaurant with the bump. I couldn't explain the bump to him. He would think it was about Melinda and the aphid, about himself. He would think it was pathetic, unbearably sad. I returned to the car.

Len texted, *Where are you*

I folded myself into the back seat and slipped out of the bump's harness, crouched as if I were engaged in some secret, sneaky behavior like changing my pants or fucking. I tugged the bump gently from beneath my sweater.

Len texted, *You coming?*

I buckled the bump into the back seat. Not to protect it, but because I couldn't leave it loose in the seat, tossed into the rear of the car with all the other forgotten, unwanted items collected in transit.

Without the bump, my sweater hung almost to my knees. Agonizing flatness. Barrenness. I nearly climbed back in the car, plastered the bump back to my body, and drove away. But Len, too, needed me, was waiting for me like a boy inside and would feel a boy's embarrassment if I failed to show.

"I'll be right back," I said to the bump. I tapped the window twice in farewell.

Len looked up, relieved, when I paused at his table. "Thought you'd stood me up," he said.

Dinner was talk of his job and Melinda and the aphid. I tried to tell him about my life—about Julie and the MotherCoders and Nana—but every story I began led me back to the bump and so had to be left unfinished. My side of the conversation withered, the bump too central to my life to be easily navigated around.

After dinner, he suggested we walk along the BeltLine. That would mean hours more away from the bump, hours more spent flat and empty out in public where anyone could see me, where someone from work could see me. I suggested he come back to my place instead. If I was to be without the bump I would rather be at home, unseen. I led him to my car, walking quickly to arrive before him. I checked on the bump, unclipped the seat belt fastened around it that seemed, in Len's presence, to be indefensibly precious. I tossed a blanket over the bump, hiding it from him.

I didn't expect him to notice the bump. He never noticed anything in the car except the speed I was driving and the cup holders, if they were full, which would inhibit his drinking of an after-work beer. But on that drive, he decided he needed more leg room, and when he tried to put his seat back the mechanism jammed, and he insisted over my protestations on taking his seat belt off while we flew seventy-five down the highway to figure out what had jammed it.

He got up on his knees on the passenger seat. I put both hands on the wheel and said, "You'll go through the windshield. I slam on the brakes right now for any reason, and you go right through the windshield. Is that what you want?"

"What's this?" He dug around behind his seat until it slid back all the way with a jolt that made him curse, slip sideways onto the center console.

"What's this?" he said again, sitting back in the passenger seat with the bump, tired and worn as a child's doll, cradled in his hands. It felt like he had his hands on my belly, inside my belly, like he was mucking around with the organs there.

"It's a pregnancy belly," I said. I didn't blush.

"Is it yours?"

"Whose else would it be?"

He laughed. "I've always wanted to wear one of these. Melinda told me to get one a few times when she was in the thick of it."

"I don't want you to try it on," I said, attempting to head him off, because he was already tugging at the back belt, slipping the patched shoulder strap over his arm.

"She didn't think I was sufficiently empathetic, Melinda."

"Don't try it on." He was working the old, beloved belt apart, looking at the fuzzy, mashed Velcro.

"You just strap it around your middle?"

"Please don't put it on."

"Why not?"

"It's not for you," I said. I took it from him, tried to shove it under the back seat, out of his reach. The car swerved, and he braced himself against the dash and said, "Watch the road."

He recovered the belly from the back seat.

"It's broken," I said.

"That's okay. We're just having fun."

I sat silently, eyes only on the road ahead while he strapped the belly on over his button-down shirt. It looked absurd there, bare, cut off from the body.

He stretched and folded his arms behind his head, pleased with himself. When we pulled up to my apartment and stepped out of the car he said, "Take a photo? For Melinda." He fished his cell phone from his pocket, reaching awkwardly past the bump.

"It's dark," I said, but he was finding his pose—leaning on the hood of the car sideways, so the bump was visible, flashing a thumbs-up. A couple walking by grinned at us. Silly. They thought we were being silly the way people infatuated with each other are silly. I nearly reached over and tore the bump off him. Instead, I took his photo for Melinda—the bump, and his grin, and behind him the car and the night, a live photo in which the bump almost seemed to move.

Inside, Nana was playing double solitaire with a neighbor-friend who doted on her. Len, who was exasperated by Nana, who had told me multiple times that I should move Nana into assisted living, strutted past the women, hamming it up. They paused their game to grin and congratulate him, saying they wished they'd had a man who'd agree to take turns. And who, they asked, was the father?

In my bedroom, he showed me the text Melinda had sent in response to the photo of the bump—three laughing-with-tears emojis.

When the ache of the back belt got to be too much for Len, he took the bump off and handed it to me. I went to put it away in my closet, but he stopped me with a hand on my arm. "Don't you want to wear it? Isn't the whole point of having it to wear it?"

"I don't want to wear it tonight."

"Come on. I want to see you in it."

Once, I, too, had wanted him to see me in it. I remembered wanting that, a remembering so strong I could nearly convince myself I wanted to wear it tonight, for Len, that this whole thing had been my idea from the start.

I put it on in the bathroom, closing the door against him, extra careful with the shoulder strap. When I came out, he whistled, and I almost took it right off again, but he came to me, put his hands on the bump, and I could feel the vibration of his touch through the silicone, as if my nerves had extended into the bump, as if he was touching me.

I wore it as we watched two episodes of *Girls Get Arrested*. Downstairs, Nana's friend washed the plates, ran the disposal, saw Nana to her bedroom, and let herself out the front door.

I felt different in the bump—because it was broken or because I was in front of him. It no longer felt a part of me. It was a prop, something to make him laugh, something for him to look at, and I wore it as we had sex, me telling him be careful, it's fragile, but still by the time we'd finished, the shoulder strap had popped again and a tear had started in the back belt, and only the adhesive of sweat and silicone kept the bump suctioned against my body, and I got to thinking about the way this all would end.

I'd always known, I think, how it would end, but as I lay beside Len, the knowing became definite. I would take a week off work in my seventh month. I would return with a flat abdomen and circles under my eyes, and no one would ask what happened or ask me to confirm. No one would say anything at all. Maybe Julie would circulate a card—something vague and reserved—*Our sympathies*. I tried to position this as a hopeful scenario.

Still, I felt not hopeful, but overwhelmingly lonely, a loneliness intensified by Len gone to sleep on his stomach beside me in the bed. I stood, holding the bump against myself with one hand, and I made my way downstairs with it, bent, clutching my abdomen in a sort of agony, like I was holding onto a limb irreparably hewn from my body, unable yet to admit it was gone for good. I made my way through the empty house to Nana's room.

There I allowed the bump to fall, peel away from my skin onto the floor with a gentle bounce, inert, useless as a beetle on its back. I said, "Nana? You asleep?"

She hmmed, groggy. "Who's that?"

"It's Louie. It's your grandbaby."

"My grandbaby. I must be getting old."

She was disoriented at night, she always was. Her mind returned her to her childhood. She scooted herself to the side and lifted the blanket for me, and I slid in beside her, on top of the crinkly absorbent pads. She said, "Where have you been, Gooch? You're pretty late getting home, aren't you? You better have a story for me in the morning or I'll tell Mama you've been with the boys."

I turned, and I cupped her, and I sobbed three sobs, which she felt in me, and she stroked my arm with her cold, corded hand, and she said, "One of them break your heart?" with the keen interest of a younger sibling.

I shook my head. It wasn't heartbreak I felt. It was grief.

"Mama told me if you make too many tears all at once, your eyeballs will float out of their sockets," Nana said.

In my sixth month, Julie did throw me a surprise office shower with lemon cake from the corner grocery store and reusable bubble letters strung together to spell "Congratulations." I wore the second, larger bump. My coworkers navigated around the bump to hug and congratulate me. I was happy there, with them. It didn't feel like pretending. We might have been celebrating anything.

ALTA'S PLACE

——

In Sharyn Gol, Alta told me, she blamed the cold. And it was cold. On the steppe, herdsmen wrapped the tails of their cattle with wool to keep them from stiffening and snapping in the wind. In her apartment, mare's milk froze solid in old soda bottles. Cooked rice congealed in the steamer before she could serve it. Her heating had not been turned on.

She rolled shortbread as she spoke. I drank milk tea and listened.

Alta told the landlord in Sharyn Gol that the cold caused her to sleep with the other woman on a single cot. The cold explained the blanket of camel hair, and the cold explained their closeness under the blanket. Cousins, she said. This is what the women had said when they rented the apartment.

The landlord must have suspected them. Why else come for the rent at dawn and on a Saturday? Why else open the door without knocking, with one key from his ring of keys?

When he entered, Alta wrapped the camel blanket around herself and rose from the cot to make tea. The other woman did not rise. The other woman did not offer explanation. She sat on the cot in her undershirt.

The landlord watched the woman in the camel blanket. The landlord accepted the rent money and a cup of tea. When Alta asked about the heating, he said the heaters would come on in two weeks, on the first day of winter, as they did every year. He finished his tea. He left.

The next month, the landlord left a notice on her apartment door. The landlord's daughter and her new husband required a place to live. There was no longer an apartment available for the two women.

Of this much, at least, Alta managed to convince the adjudicator at the asylum office in Arlington, Virginia. She did not have the notice to show him. She'd been just nineteen then, not yet in the habit of keeping things.

"Now, I keep them," she said when she told me this story. She gestured to her filing cabinet, where she kept copies of every lease, every credit card statement, every Costco receipt and bus ticket stub.

The landlord gave them time to sort their belongings, to find another place. But he must have spoken about them to the woman who owned apartments in the Hedde District and the manager at the Arig Complex, because when Alta called there were no vacancies. So she slept, again, on the couch in her parents' three-room apartment, on a pillow stuffed with her baby clothes. Above her bed, her grandmother's wedding deel was pinned to the wall for luck.

I was alone the night Alta came to the Snow White Launderers in Arlington. The pants presser and the manager had gone home. I was drawing in my sketch journal, practicing my patterning. Back then, I sketched dresses with eyelet lace and scalloped hems. I sketched dresses I couldn't afford to make, dresses for high occasions.

She entered in a two-piece gingham suit—skirt and jacket with a wide check print and a stain darkening the right sleeve. It was December. Gingham is a summer fabric, but I didn't mention that.

"What happened?" I asked her. As a countergirl, it was my job to elicit a thorough case history, separate the brown of dried blood from the brown of honey mustard, determine whether hydrogen peroxide or a detergent stick would better lift the stain.

"I gave an interview," she said.

"Sure, but what happened?" I motioned to her suit.

"Coffee," she said. "Can you clean it?"

"I can't clean it while you're wearing it."

I pointed her to the shabby bathroom where the pants presser, on rainy days, spent her smoke break exhaling into the cooling vent. I asked if she'd need a change of clothes. We had two men's shirts and a trench coat in our discard pile, waiting for the Goodwill truck.

She said she had a change with her, though she wasn't carrying anything but a briefcase so thin I'd guessed it empty.

At that time, I'd been working at the dry cleaner's less than a month, the evening shift, two to eight. I thought it would be just a summer gig. I'd studied fashion design, and I was looking for a foot in the door. Dry cleaning wasn't quite that, but I could handle fabrics daily, gain experience with durability and stain resistance, pay rent on my one-room efficiency in Arlington.

She emerged from the bathroom in a garment of blue silk—a robe, I thought, but it wasn't a robe. It was contoured, gownlike but not a gown. Not a wrap dress, though the belt suggested it. An ancestor of wrap dresses, perhaps. It felt that way—historic, significant, organic in its delicacy, like a moth fresh-sprung from chrysalis. It had no seams I could see. No buttons or zippers. Just a catch of silk at her throat and a cut-cloth sash at her waist.

I'd seen one-piece clothing on the New York runways, one-piece jumpsuits from Cédric Charlier, origami dresses from Issey Miyake cut and folded from a single piece of cloth. Even their best attempts allowed for zippers, a blind hem. Her garment had no fastenings. The cloth clung to her shoulders of its own accord, held there by static or gravity.

I took the gingham suit, which she had folded neatly. "Is it one cloth?" I asked.

She thought I meant the suit. She reached for it, to check. The suit was my professional responsibility. I should have asked about the suit, but I had eyes only for the garment she wore. I gestured with my hand, almost touching her. "What you're wearing."

"It's a deel," she said.

I was polite. I didn't ask where it was from, where she was from. Instead, as I tagged her suit, I asked what else she needed.

She needed Vaseline. The coffee had splashed on her wrist. Her skin was pink there. I didn't have Vaseline, but I offered her lip balm. I told her she should complain about the coffee. It shouldn't be hot enough to burn.

"The problem isn't the coffee," she said, gliding the lip balm across her skin.

"Then what's the problem?" I asked.

She pulled the sleeve of the deel down over the burn. The grease in the lip balm would rub off on the deel, leaving a small colorless stain. When she noticed the stain, maybe she would bring the deel to me.

In the interview, she had told them she was a lesbian. This was the reason she'd left Mongolia. When she said it, the interviewer stood. He poured coffee for himself, then offered her some. She accepted, though she drank coffee only rarely and never black. When he leaned over the desk with her cup, she thought he was handing it to her. He was planning to set it on the desk. Their hands collided, and the coffee spilled.

"Why didn't he hand it to me?" she asked me in the dry cleaner's, returning my lip balm.

"Maybe he was worried the cup was too hot?"

She shook her head. "He didn't want to touch me. He didn't want to touch my hand."

"No," I said. "I'm sure it wasn't that." She waited, but I didn't elaborate. Our hands hadn't touched when she returned my lip balm. I wished they had. I offered to deliver her suit when it was finished, though this was against company policy.

She accepted. She wrote her address in blue pen at the top of her laundry receipt and gathered her briefcase. She told me her name was Altansharzam. She said I could call her Alta.

My name was Cory. "I'm a lesbian, too," I said, in part because I suspected it was true, and in part because it was my habit, then, to remember what had been said and reflect it back to the speaker as if it were an invention of my own.

"That's nice for you," Alta said. And she was gone.

After she left, I traded my 4B drawing pencil for a lighter one, and I sketched her from memory. I focused on capturing the deel—its lines, its corded hem. I didn't sketch Alta's hands, her bitten fingernails. I didn't sketch her braid. I left her face just a three-line profile, left off the sunspot beneath her right eye, left off her mouth, which was quick to lift at the corners. I thought of her for the rest of my shift—not Alta the person but Alta the sketch, made more vibrant by the drab background of the laundry.

If I could sketch her now, I'd sketch every detail of that face, those hands, keep her close to me that way.

Alta lived with a woman. Oyuka. I met her by accident, my first time in their apartment. I knocked, and she called, "Come in."

I opened the door and looked for Alta. Alta reading a novel. Alta playing the harp. But Alta wasn't there.

"Who is it?" Oyuka called.

I said, "Dry cleaning."

The apartment was typical, a one-bedroom with a narrow balcony overlooking the street and an odor of electric heat and cooking oil. Disappointing. I took my time entering, noting the coat closet and the boy's bike, a stack of foundation powders in different skin tones. I let one finger brush the handle of an umbrella, the umbrella Alta must carry, her hand wrapped around the plastic crook. I passed a table with a half-finished puzzle, and that's when I saw Oyuka. She sat in the bedroom in a ladder-back chair, working a newspaper crossword. A catheter tube extended from beneath her skirt into a wide-rimmed bowl. She was a little older than Alta. Maybe thirty. She said, "You'll excuse me. I'd need a leg bag to get to the door," and lifted the end of her catheter from the bowl to show me.

"Dry cleaning for Alta," I said.

"Set it on the table there."

"It's for Alta."

"She's not here."

"Will she be back soon?"

"She's getting my boy from school."

"She's expecting me with her suit."

"I'll be sure she gets it."

When I made no move to leave, she said, "Do we owe you?"

I could wait, I said. Alta might have other clothing that needed cleaning.

"I don't know when she'll be back."

"When does she usually get back?" I could stay. I could wait for Alta. I had nothing else to do with my day.

"I don't know when she'll be back," Oyuka said again. I considered that Oyuka might be Alta's partner, then dismissed the possibility. Oyuka had none of Alta's intrigue. She was dressed practically, her hair pulled into a loose ponytail, no makeup, clothes chosen for comfort not cut.

"I do pickups," I said, though pickups were also against

company policy. "Do you have anything, any evening wear that needs cleaning?"

"There might be a pair of pants hanging in the closet there."

With her permission, I drew back the closet's accordion doors. There, beside the linen pants, on a cushioned hanger, hung the deel.

"Not that one," the woman said when I put my hand on the deel's pleated sleeve, lightly stained on the inner cuff, just as I'd expected. "She wouldn't want you taking that one."

"No," I said, but I snaked my arm up through the sleeve, cuff to shoulder. I curled my fingers over the collar and fingered the silk knots for fastening. I felt I had found Alta, unsuspecting and vulnerable, tucked away among the coats.

I left with the pants draped over my arm and promised to return.

For three months, I went weekly to Alta's apartment. I went for her dry cleaning, though mostly there was no dry cleaning. Alta refused my offer to wash the small grease stain from the deel. She preferred to wash even silks herself. I went to her apartment anyway. I stayed as long as she allowed me to stay.

Alta often added peppercorns to black tea and steeped it in milk for Oyuka's son, Bat, who drank it crouched beside the baseboard heater. Alta had a whole butchered sheep delivered to her apartment by a farmer out of Reston. Alta owned a set of knucklebones with which you could play a game like dominoes. I asked her to teach me the game, but she preferred to play solitaire with a card deck.

I didn't see Oyuka for a while. Sometimes I heard her through the walls, a snatch of laughter or song. Once, Alta also paused to listen. "Oyuka's dancing," she said. But the bedroom door was always closed. I saw no one, not even Alta, enter that room.

I asked Alta to introduce me to Oyuka, formally. I wanted to understand their relationship. She said Oyuka's parents had come to America from Mongolia when Oyuka was eleven years old. Oyuka was a teacher. She'd had a stroke a year ago. Alta kept her company after, kept her company still.

"Does she go out?"

"To church," Alta said. "Sometimes."

"Anywhere else?"

"I do her cooking. You do her laundry. Where is she needing to go?"

It bothered me, some. I thought Alta was keeping me from Oyuka or keeping Oyuka from me, embarrassed by one of us.

Nothing Alta said suggested romance, and I thought surely Alta, who had flown halfway around the world, wouldn't choose a woman who never left her room.

"Does she have guests?" I asked. "Don't you open the door?"

"After work, I will open it," Alta said, but Alta was always working.

From her front room, Alta sold things. She sold watermelon pickled in old mayonnaise jars. She sold shortbread at the zakh on Saturdays. She stamped each loaf with a woodcut, called it shoe-bottom bread. She sold Maybelline cosmetics. For twenty dollars, she offered two-hour private lessons in shading and contouring, products not included.

Alta's customers didn't make appointments. When Alta was home, she hung a sign from her porch—"Alta's Place for a New Face"—and the Mongolian women came. Alta seated them in one wicker-backed chair and wiped the skin around their eyes with a milk-soaked cotton ball. She asked about their families as she pecked with tweezers at their eyebrows. If a woman's eyes watered in pain, Alta smothered the tears with her thumb. She said, "We'll need that cheek dry."

They leaned in to Alta as if to a mirror. She painted her face, stroke by stroke, and they copied her. They cringed when she wet her thumb to wipe away their clumsy contouring.

In my sketch pad, I copied her, too. I sat on the couch beside Bat. Bat's favorite T-shirt had "Virginia Is for Farmers" printed across the chest. He liked it because it was large enough he could pull his arms and legs inside. Alta called it his turtle look. He peeked over my shoulder as I sketched the women. In life, they wore button-downs and boatneck dresses. In my sketchbook, they wore deels.

At the lesson's end, they blinked at Alta with eyes made large, her twin. They sipped black tea and exclaimed over the lipstick, which left no stain on teacup or teeth, and which Alta sold for fourteen dollars. They left with a tube or two, and she washed their face from hers, stored her products on the middle rack of her convection oven, and waited to begin again.

Alta always sent me home with her last student. "Cory," she

would say, "Yuna is going to see Shakespeare in the park. Maybe that is interesting for you." She said the same about an all-you-can-eat pasta buffet and a beginner guitar lesson and even a dentist appointment. *Maybe that is interesting for you,* she said and left me to walk home beside her students. On those walks, I asked about Alta. Where had Alta studied cosmetology? Her students laughed. In her bedroom, in her mirror.

I asked about deels. I had read about them. I had memorized the sequence of Cyrillic characters that denoted the garment—дээл. I paused on one walk with a student to carefully write the characters on my sketch pad for her approval. Was it true, I asked another, that people kept special items in the front of their deels, in the pouch above the belt? Was it true that both men and women wore deels? Yes, they said. That's true.

I never asked Alta's students about Oyuka. I believed Oyuka was a secret Alta trusted only to a few. When one student mentioned that Alta looked tired, I thought of Alta making dinner for Oyuka late in the evening, helping Oyuka into bed, Oyuka needing so much from Alta. I said nothing. The secret of Oyuka was safe with me.

By the new year, Alta and I were at ease with each other. Once, Alta even forgot about me. Her last student had gone home. She was rolling out the dough of her shortbread to sell at the zakh the next day. I had often imagined the zakh, a Mongolian zakh, where Alta spent Saturdays selling watermelon and shortbread. I pictured a crowded square, like a festival, the people in deels pushing wooden carts through shady, cobbled streets and shouting in Mongolian.

Of course, the zakh wouldn't be like this. It was in Arlington, just down the street from a grocery store and a taco stand. But Alta often met other Mongolian women there—that was one reason she went—so I wanted to see it. I wanted Alta to introduce me to those women. "This is my friend Cory," she would say.

I called Alta's name from my seat on her couch. I said, "Can I go with you to the zakh tomorrow?"

Alta startled. "I thought you were gone," she said.

This didn't bother me. It matched my vision of intimacy, to sit silently in the corner of someone else's life until she stopped noticing.

"Can I go with you tomorrow?"

"You are like my husband," Alta said. "Sitting. Watching me."

"Your husband? You were married?"

"I told him, you have time to watch, you have time to help."

"Can I help at the zakh? I've never been to a zakh."

"Maybe one day," Alta said. She said the same thing when Bat asked her to shave his head or to visit the trampoline stadium. "Maybe one day." A polite but clear refusal.

At my next visit, I asked Alta about her husband. I thought she'd brush the question off, evade it as she had done before. Instead, as she washed eye shadow samples from the crest of her thumb, she said, "My husband was like Oyuka—always telling me bring this, do that. When I am a wifey wife, he was happy, she is happy, just the same."

Alta kept her marriage certificate and her wedding deel. She brought them to her asylum interview. She brought her passport. Form I-94. Form I-589, a copy. Five credit cards, including Shell, Kohl's, and Fingerhut. She studied Yelp reviews for the top-ten gay bars in Arlington.

In January, I found the printed Yelp reviews in the drawer beneath her oven. I asked her about them. She told me she had heard stories. She had heard of women denied asylum because they couldn't list local gay locations, because they weren't part of the lesbian community, because they'd only ever paid with cash.

She subscribed to *Curve* and *Pride Life* to be safe. Old issues of the magazines, sorted alphabetically, filled the lowest drawer of her filing cabinet. When she got the February issues she filed them away. I knelt with her beside the cabinet. "You can take them with you if you want," she said.

"Have you read them?" I asked her. I removed one magazine at random. On the cover, a woman stood wearing lingerie in front of an open refrigerator.

"They are kind of difficult for me."

So I read them. I sat on her sofa and read about the five types of lesbians and about women who were triple-bi—biracial, bicultural, bisexual. I was not bi-anything and felt this as something of a lack. I thought of Alta as bisexual, married for years to a man, though I never asked her if this was true.

At twenty-three, romance so far for me was standing as fit model for Bailey Watts twelve hours before her senior thesis show, holding the exhale as her hands bumped my ribs, pinning skirt to bodice for an empire waist. Or asking my studio partner to model my linen tunic, lifting her hair and cinching the keyhole neckline with satin ribbon. Or perhaps lying on my back on the sand of Virginia Beach—where my family rented for one week each winter a house right on the water—lying at the tide line, alone, shivering as the waves broke over my belly.

I read the magazines with an avidity that bothered Alta. She distracted me. She asked me questions about the United States—Who did the makeup for the actors on Broadway? Why didn't Americans eat sheep? She was still waiting to hear about her asylum application, and once she asked me how long after interviewing she would have to wait. I googled this with enthusiasm. I told her it could take three months to a year, or longer. I expected dismay, but Alta nodded. She was confirming a timeline she'd already known. Her questions were unnecessary, like the tasks she gave me—helping Bat through third-grade math, spinning the small drums of her prayer wheels, slicing apples for Bat's father, who came on Friday afternoons and expected to be fed. Bat's father stood in the doorway of Oyuka's bedroom, eating the watermelon Alta had pickled to sell, and told Oyuka Bat needed a drum set. If Oyuka could afford live-in help, he said, she could afford a drum set.

"He is a fool," Alta said to me. "He thinks I am sleeping every night on the couch."

I looked away from Alta, at my fingers on the wrinkled corners of her magazines. I did not tell her that when I thought of her in the empty spaces of those weeks, I also imagined her sitting in the evenings in the front room in her blue deel, watching *Jeopardy* for the English practice, spooning globes of oil from the surface of her soup. I also imagined her alone.

In Ulaanbaatar, a city of one million people, Alta had known no one. She'd moved to the city with her husband, because the jobs in the city were better. Even her husband she didn't know. They'd been married only two months.

"I was a lonely person," she said, as I helped her strip white slipcovers from her couch.

The roads were better in the city. The schools and theaters were better. The air was worse. Alta wore a mask, which fit tight as a palm over her nose and mouth. She was supposed to keep the windows of their apartment closed at all times, so the air inside would be safe to breathe. She refused. She liked the breeze through the windows. She liked the chill. She liked to watch crystals of ice form on the window panes.

In late fall, her husband caulked the windows, preventing her opening them. This was usual, necessary to keep the apartment warm in winter. He assured her there was plenty of air through the ventilation shafts, but sometimes she sat at the dining table in the late mornings, alone, and worked just to breathe.

She asked her husband every day when they would return to Sharyn Gol, where she could tell cattle apart by the clip of their ears and had family to visit on the weekends, a life of her own.

When we'd finished folding the slipcovers, she asked me, "What about your family?"

Her question surprised me. I'd told my family about Alta, my friend Alta. When they called to catch up, it was her life I described in detail. I'd begun saying medegui when my mother asked about my future. мэдэхгүй translates to I don't know, but to me the word conveyed more—not just I don't know, but How should I know? Why are you asking me?

I'd never told Alta about my family. Alta rarely asked questions, and I volunteered little. What was there to tell? My mother was a divorce attorney. My father sold credit card readers to big-box stores. They announced their divorce the month I turned eighteen. They'd been planning it for years, waiting for my high school graduation. My mother called my job a dead end. We didn't talk often.

"We're not close," I said.

"But your mother? You visit her?"

I shrugged. The last time I'd visited my mother, I'd told her I was gay. I thought it would be good for her. She was vaguely Christian, vaguely conservative. Not a bad person. She prayed for gays, but never protested them, believed protest of any kind to be wasted effort. She didn't cry when I told her. She didn't shout or leave the room. She told me a story about a woman couple from her church who'd gone on mission to Africa and decided somewhere near Tanzania they weren't lesbians. They were just wounded in their hearts. Take your time, my mother said to me, deciding about those things.

To Alta I said, "My mother doesn't understand."

Alta shook her head. "Your mother didn't ask if you were gay, Cory. No one asked you."

"I'm not going to wait until they ask," I said.

"It's nice for you," Alta said. "It's nice no one is asking." Alta put her fingers to the wrinkles beneath her eyes, looking not at me but into her mirror, at her skin loose and bare of powder.

"Sorry," I said.

"Why are you sorry?" Alta said.

I didn't know how to answer her, and she didn't wait for an answer. She piled the slipcovers into my arms along with a comforter. The comforter smelled of urine. As I took it from her, I felt insulted.

Those were the last items I dry-cleaned for Alta.

In late spring, the asylum office made its decision. Alta should return to Mongolia. She could live in Ulaanbaatar. According to the country reports, the Mongolian city was more tolerant than the countryside. Alta could be discreet there. She could be safe. They had found insufficient evidence of persecution, insufficient reason for fear. Alta's asylum claim hadn't been denied, but it had been referred to immigration court. She would need to attend a hearing there.

Alta told me this at the dry cleaner's, the day after I left her apartment with the slipcovers. She'd come to pick them up but they weren't ready. She knew they wouldn't be ready. She came to see me, I think, to tell me her news.

I took my break right away. I led Alta outside and around to the back of the cleaner's, where the hum of the air conditioner would ensure our privacy.

The pants presser was finishing her smoke break. I expected we'd wait for the pants presser to leave, but Alta didn't wait.

"It is impossible," Alta said. "I can't go back to the city."

"You won't go back," I said. "We won't let that happen."

But I felt a pulse of dread, as if Alta was already leaving, leaving me.

The pants presser lit a cigarette for Alta. Alta thanked her. I wished I'd thought of a cigarette. I didn't know how to be with Alta in front of the pants presser. I'd only ever been with Alta in her apartment—not in the street in the sun in front of people I knew.

"They could use you inside, up front," I said to the presser. Leave. Go away.

"I've got another five minutes," the presser said.

"I left the city," Alta said. Before coming to the States, she'd returned with her husband to Sharyn Gol, where her husband worked winters in the Canadian mine, one of the better mines. He worked summers in South Korea. In Sharyn Gol, the woman with the camel blanket—

"I've always wanted to travel to South Korea," the presser said, "South Korea or Japan." The presser was an idiot. The presser didn't understand. Alta had news. Alta's life and my life by extension were tipping, tipping, even as the presser said, "I've heard the food's better in South Korea, which you wouldn't expect."

The presser and Alta talked about kimchi. Alta made her own. Alta knew where the presser could get kochukaru by the pound.

The presser stubbed out her cigarette with maddening slowness. "Thanks for the tip," she said, and Alta nodded, impossibly composed, impossibly generous.

When the presser left, I said, urgently, "The woman with the camel blanket. What about her?"

But Alta had taken a receipt from her purse and was writing on it with a pen, writing down the address of a Korean market, giving this to me to pass along to the presser.

"The camel blanket," I said, shoving the receipt into my pocket. "The woman."

In Sharyn Gol, Alta met the woman with the camel blanket again. The woman hadn't married. She taught chemistry at school number four. While Alta's husband was living in South Korea in the summers, she slept in the bed in Alta's apartment, which they had to themselves.

That woman told her sister. Her sister could be trusted. Perhaps it wasn't the sister. Perhaps it was the man who cleared trash from the apartment's stairwell. Or a neighbor watching from the flat across the square. Alta didn't know. It was September when she lost her job. She was twenty-five. Her husband came home from South Korea on an evening she'd sliced tsuivan noodles for dinner and asked if it was true she'd shared his bed with a woman. She tried at first to tell him it wasn't true.

She went to her grandparents in the countryside. She lived in a good felt tent beside their home. Mornings and evenings, she took milk from their Kalmyk cows and curdled it over a woodstove, sold the sweet curds. She told time by the contrails of jets that nosed across her sky. At two o'clock, the Beijing-to-Moscow direct swinging northwest. At six in the evening, the Moscow-to-Incheon freight slicing the blue the other way.

In her interview, they'd asked, Was it true that he had come to her grandparents' home? Her husband had come to find her?

But that part was not important.

Of course, it was important, I said. I needed her to continue. I needed to know the story, the whole story. All of it was important, I said.

Her husband was not among the things she was afraid of.

What was she afraid of? I asked her.

She was afraid the court would not believe she was in danger. She was afraid the court would refuse to grant her asylum.

But in Mongolia, I said. In Mongolia, what was she afraid of?

She shared with me the words she had found in an encyclopedia of social work. She practiced them with me, remembering not to hold the vowels too long, remembering *s* can be soft like *switch* or have a buzz like *scissors*, remembering to keep it soft when she says *economic persecution*, to buzz just lightly in the center of *housing*—then soft—*discrimination*. She could use the English she learned in secondary school—*I can't get a job. I can't get an apartment.* But she wanted the real words, the right words.

What else? I said. I had words. I had plenty of words.

She didn't need more words.

She did, I countered. Obviously, she did, or they'd have granted her claim.

Silence from Alta. She dropped her cigarette to the pavement, stepped on it. "It's not like that. It's not my fault. You can't predict these things."

"A lawyer could."

"But you are not a lawyer. You work here." Alta pointed to the laundry.

I was silent. Stunned. She might as well have slapped me.

"I should go," Alta said. "Oyuka is waiting."

"Oyuka will be fine," I said. "You do too much for her." Let Oyuka wait, let her wait all day.

"It's a difficult day for Oyuka. A difficult day for both of us."

But I didn't want to think about Oyuka. "What happened to the woman with the camel blanket?" I asked. I needed to know what would happen to Alta if she went back.

She is not allowed to teach. She has no work. She has to live with her sister.

But had anyone hurt her? Had she been harmed?

Alta shook her head like closing a door.

"You can tell me," I said. "You can tell me anything."

"You sound like them," Alta said, "asking these questions."

"Like who?"

"The interviewers. The ones at the asylum office."

A contraction of my stomach, as in response to cold water. "I'm your friend," I said. "I'm not interviewing you." When I thought of asylum interviewers, I thought of white men with gray hair and a paunch at their gut, just there for the paycheck.

"You're always asking questions, Mongolia, Mongolia."

"I'm not asking about Mongolia. I'm asking about you," I said. "If you don't want to talk about Mongolia, just say so."

"I don't want to talk about it."

"Fine," I said. "We'll talk about something else." But I couldn't in that moment think of anything else to say to Alta.

"Tomorrow, I will go to sell my shortbread at the zakh," Alta said into my silence. "You still want to come?"

I did. Of course I did.

"Tomorrow, you can come."

I understood her sudden offer as a final opportunity, a last chance.

"You're not going to leave," I said. In my voice, a quiver—terror, terror at the thought of a life without Alta, a life that was wholly my own. "I don't even know what to wear. I don't have anything to wear to a zakh."

"You can wear your street clothes."

"Will you wear the deel?"

"I'll wear my street clothes."

"Can I wear the deel?" I waited, breath held, for her answer to both the direct question and a deeper question—Did she trust me? Was I an American friend worthy of her deel?

Alta considered me. "Maybe if you want, you can wear it," she said. "Maybe it is interesting for you."

Her agreement didn't make me feel how I expected—no surge of excitement, no elation. I would wear the deel. I didn't have it in me to decline, but I felt a rising dread. I sensed, in her acquiescence, a farewell, and I understood for the first time that whether Alta remained in the States or left for Mongolia, we would not be lifelong friends. Alta knew this. Alta had always known.

Alta was wearing, that day, a breezy white blouse tucked into tight black jeans. I remember, because I told myself to remember. I told myself this might be one of the last times I saw Alta, and I watched her walk out of that alley, noticing her jeans were cuffed at the ankles, memorizing the exact way the cuffs brushed her ankles until the air-conditioning unit blocked her from view.

That wasn't the last time I saw Alta. I saw her the very next day, but when I think about her leaving, this is what I see.

The next morning, at Alta's apartment, I apologized to her. No more questions, I promised.

"It's fine," Alta said, impatient as she always was with my apologies.

She helped me into the deel. She said I could leave my blouse and leggings and wear the deel over them, but I wanted to wear it the right way, as she would wear it. I wanted the silk against my skin. So Alta held the deel like a curtain between us and waited for me to undress and step into it, thread my arms through the pleated sleeves, fill them.

As I stepped into the deel, I realized it wasn't one piece of fabric. An inner seam joined the front and back, but I registered no disappointment, because Alta was fastening the sleeves and the bodice around me, her hands working the knots deftly just centimeters from my skin.

She must dress Oyuka each morning just like this, buttoning her collared shirts, Alta's knuckles brushing Oyuka's chest. My cheeks went hot. Arousal and shame. Shame that I was aroused, which felt like a betrayal of Alta, of our friendship. Shame at the deel, my body in it, which felt also like betrayal, though I had asked Alta. Alta had agreed.

"I've been researching immigration hearings," I said. I'd spent the night watching videos. Videos posted by nonprofits and shared with #refugeerights #valuetranslives. "You should wear a men's suit to your hearing," I said. Women wore men's suits in the videos. A woman from Uganda wore a bowler hat and a men's button-down. A woman from Russia shaved one side of her head and cut her fingernails down to the bed. A man from Brazil considered appearing at his interview in drag, but settled finally for a pink-collared shirt and matching eye shadow.

"I will wear eye shadow," she said. "And my suit."

"You should wear a men's suit," I said. "At least a pantsuit."

But she had bought the suit especially for these interviews. "It's a good suit."

"You should wear the deel," I said.

Alta huffed. "It's too small. It's not comfortable for me."

"I can make you one, a larger one." We could fly the silk in express from Mongolia. Alta could watch me while I sewed. I could help her. "I'll make you a deel to wear."

"It's not comfortable for me," Alta said. "They know I'm Mongolian. I don't need the deel."

"This is different," I said. "Look," I said to Alta. I looked at myself in her makeup mirror, and the shame vanished. In the deel I looked not like myself. I remembered that both men and women wore deels. Men's deels were different, but I didn't know the differences. I didn't know anything at all about deels, and this ignorance meant that I looked, in the deel, like a tiny, delicate man. An emperor. No, a woman dressed like an emperor, in an emperor's costume.

"All night, I made shortbread for the two of us to carry and sell," Alta said. "If we sell all the shortbread, next Saturday I will have a rest day."

"Let me make a deel for you. A deel that fits you."

"This court tells everyone no," Alta said, wrapping the belt of the deel beneath my ribs. "I've heard this."

She cinched the belt tight. My breath circled in my chest. "Where will you go?" I asked Alta. If she couldn't stay here, where would she go?

She knew a place outside Sharyn Gol. She had slept in this place once for four days in the winter. She would go there.

I didn't say I would go with her, would visit her. It was too early to say those things. There was still a chance Alta would stay.

Alta went to the bedroom door, the door that was always closed. She opened it. "The shortbread is in the bedroom."

The bedroom. Their bedroom. Where I'd never been invited to go.

Alta said, "Come in, Cory."

I walked to the door and paused. In the bedroom, Bat's army men were scattered beneath a card table. His clothes hung over the drying line nearest the radiator. Books and DVDs towered against the far wall. Six watermelons lolled beneath the window. Bat sat on one watermelon, rolling slowly back and forth, dropping a plastic parachute man from hand to hand.

Oyuka sat in her ladder-back chair, looked at me in the deel, and said, "What's the occasion?"

"Cory thinks I should interview like that," Alta said. Then somehow both women were laughing. Bat glanced up and grinned, unsurprised. I was surprised. I stood in the doorway, not knowing how to stand in the deel, where to put my hands. I watched them. I couldn't remember ever hearing Alta laugh.

"She'll be a sight at the farmers' market," Oyuka said.

"Cory doesn't mind attention."

One end of the deel's belt had unraveled and was tickling my left calf. I caught it. I tried to tuck it back in without Alta noticing, embarrassed the belt had come undone, as if the deel itself rejected me. "You said it was a zakh," I said. "We're going to a zakh."

"A zakh is a market," said Alta. "A market is a zakh." Alta knelt beside the card table, stacking her shortbread in produce boxes—one for me, one for her.

The zakh was the farmers' market. She'd been talking all along about the farmers' market. "I can't wear this to the farmers' market," I said. The belt unraveled again. I gathered up the tail end in my hand, annoyed with the belt, annoyed with Alta. I couldn't show up at the farmers' market in a blue silk deel. Surely Alta knew that.

"You'll be a sight," Oyuka said.

"It's fine," Alta said, stacking her shortbread so high we'd have to peer out between the loaves. "Come help me, Cory," she said.

She wanted me to enter the room where Oyuka danced. Where Alta laughed. Where they slept together. There on the bed was a blanket of woven wool. There, an orange plastic bathtub propped against a child's easel. There, the empty jars to be sterilized for canning, the army fort made from a cereal box, the package of Russian butter cookies open, half-eaten. There, the room where she lived.

The room embarrassed me. I had never considered there must be more to Alta, that her life might have dimensions beyond those she'd shared with me, beyond the story I'd told about her. I was ridiculous, standing there in the deel her grandmother had made.

"Take this box to the other room, Cory," Alta said.

Alta lifted the box and walked toward me. Looking back, I think she meant to hand me the box. She expected me to place my hands beneath the corners of the box and be ready for the weight when she released it.

At the time, this wasn't clear to me. I thought she'd set the box on the floor. I'd take it from there. I couldn't take the box from her. I had the belt wrapped around my hand. I needed Alta's help with the belt, but Alta couldn't tell this, couldn't see me, because she'd stacked the loaves so high, too high, impossibly high.

Alta let go of the box. The shortbread fell.

Cascaded.

The loaves broke. Crumbs scattered beneath Oyuka's chair, into the doorway. Alta knelt and crushed one loaf beneath her knee. She lowered the box, began restacking.

Bat stole a piece from the ground and ate it.

"Those won't sell," Oyuka said. "Might as well leave them."

Alta stacked.

"Get the broom," Oyuka said.

Alta stacked. She'd started to sweat, working right up beside the radiator. She made small noises of effort. She raised her head, strands of her black hair coming loose from the braid, crushed shortbread in each hand.

"Are you going to help, Cory?" she said. "Or are you just going to look and look?"

As if I were a gawker. Some man ogling her.

Wasn't I helping her? Hadn't I tried?

I should have gone to her. I should have stacked the useless shortbread. But I couldn't bring myself to enter their bedroom, their life—not like that, not for the very first time.

I said, "I have to change," and shut the bedroom door.

I stood alone in the room where I'd thought I'd known Alta, in the room where she told her stories, practiced with me until the English words, once unfamiliar, snapped to her tongue in sequence, easy as falling to the next drum of the prayer wheels, easy as cream before foundation before blush.

I let the belt unwind completely. Alta's deel fell from me.

As I dressed, I listened for the women in the other room. I heard nothing. As if they'd gone, vanished together as soon as I'd shut the door.

I left Alta's apartment without any dry cleaning. My empty arms swung. There were no demands at all upon my person or my time. No restrictions. Nothing to wait for, nothing to dread, nothing to force me to justify my life or to change it.

I'd have folded Alta's deel if I'd known how to fold it. I didn't know, so I laid it over the arm of her couch, laid it out carefully. When Alta emerged from her room to hang the deel, it would be ready for her—no wrinkles, no stray hairs, no dampness in the armpits, no evidence I'd worn it at all.

I didn't know Alta had gone until the next fall. Oyuka called the cleaner's—"I have sweaters for dry cleaning," she said.

I held the phone with both hands. I needed to speak to Alta.

Alta had left in the summer. "I remember you did pickups."

"I'm sorry," I said. "We don't, we can't offer that service anymore."

She said she'd try another place.

"But wait," I said. "Wait. What about Alta?"

"What about her?"

"Where is she? How is she?"

She was in Ulaanbaatar.

Was she all right?

She was in Ulaanbaatar. She had family there.

But I knew better. I knew where Alta was. She was in the brick maintenance station outside Sharyn Gol, where she'd once spent four nights. She'd slept against water pipes. She'd not wanted to return to her husband, and it was winter, and the water pipes were warm.

When Alta told me this story, she had said she was alone those four nights, but I tell it my way: A boy found her there. A boy Bat's age—free enough, aimless enough to find her. He perched in the window of the maintenance station, which could be closed with wooden shutters, but could not be locked. He watched her, glee on his face at discovering her, a vicious obstinate glee. Alta knew she needed to give him something to gain his loyalty, his silence, but what? All she had in the maintenance station was mutton or curd, which wouldn't interest him, and her makeup palette. She showed him her palette, painted her face there in front of him, a peep show. He wasn't impressed. Likely, his mother had done the same a dozen times.

"You can try," Alta said. She offered him a brush. "Copy me," she said. He painted stroke after stroke just as she did, and when they'd finished they studied themselves and each other in the reflective steel of the pipe, and she saw he was afraid, a little, ashamed, a little.

Why not? Why not let it begin this way—the boy ducking quickly back through the window, and Alta watching him, the boy taking fistful after fistful of snow to scrub his face bare and pink, and Alta feeling, as she watches him, a sense of relief.

THE EXPECTATION
OF COOPER HILL

—

All my life I've been told I take after Sylvia Summer. Sylvia "Spoon" Summer. My great-great-grandmother. My namesake. I am Vee.

Sylvia Summer was a midwife. She kept her herbs and all her belongings in a two-wheeled cart, which she pulled from town to town, birth to birth. Her legs were long. She could cross any stream in two steps—one into the water and one out.

She settled in Cooper Hill, an eddy of a town on the Tennessee River, well back in the clay beds. She was there in August 1928, when another midwife named Aunt Paulina returned from some fancy training in Montgomery. Sylvia went to meet her. All the midwives of Cooper Hill did. Aunt Paulina showed them her new leather doctor's bag and the glass-bottled pharmaceuticals— silver nitrate, for the infant's eyes; boric acid, better than lard for the cord; a length of sterile linen cloth, which lined the bag's interior.

The midwives of Cooper Hill took turns carrying the leather bag up and down the street, strutting under its weight. They listened to the glass bottles chime inside. Sylvia Summer, on her turn, thumbed the clasp and opened the bag. The bag was so dark inside she couldn't see the bottom. She reached down with her fingers. Nothing. The bag went on and on forever. Sylvia reached her hand, her whole arm, her head and shoulders down into that emptiness.

Now, wait a minute.

"That's impossible," I said to my grandmother. I was thirteen.

"That's how it was."

"I don't believe it."

The leather bag smelled sour inside, like old milk. From its depths came a breath of hot air, a beery exhale. Sylvia Summer withdrew her head and shoulders. She snapped that bag shut.

One month later, according to my grandmother, Sylvia Summer vanished.

Sylvia was strong. She once took first place in the crosscut-sawing competition at the Montgomery lumberjack show. She carried a pig knife with a bone handle, and she could use it. She was large. Tall, I mean. Big-boned, like my grandmother. Sylvia Summer broke chairs, sometimes got stuck in doorways. She was often mistaken, from behind, for a man. People don't expect a woman to be so tall.

She was white, unusual for a midwife in that time. She was never trained as a midwife. Never licensed. She had no family and no home. Her only child—a boy, my great-grandfather—she left at a nunnery. She visited him once a year. She devoted her life instead to the public, delivering hundreds of babies. When she started her work, an infant come to term in rural Alabama had a one in six chance of dying before it cleared the womb—by the end of her tenure, it was down to one in ten. I'm not saying that was all her doing, but she had a part.

For two decades, she corresponded regularly with Elizabeth Cromwell, leader of women's health reform in Alabama. I always knew they'd corresponded, but for many years I hadn't read her letters. I've read them now. Sometimes I wish I hadn't read them, that I'd somehow protected the Sylvia Summer of my childhood.

My grandmother was a midwife, too. She caught her last baby in the bathtub of a Red Roof Inn. That baby got her a felony conviction.

Usually, my grandmother caught her babies across the state line in Florida, where she had a birthing house with a Jacuzzi tub and a license to practice midwifery. But that day, as she drove the mother and her husband toward the state line, a tractor trailer overturned on the highway eastbound. Three lanes of traffic gridlocked. My grandmother pulled off the highway, parked at the nearest motel. She caught that baby six miles shy of the Florida border in a rented room where the bathtub faucet only dribbled. There wasn't but an inch of water in the tub when the baby slid into my grandmother's hands—fast and headfirst and blue as lungfish, all tangled in his cord.

My grandmother spent six minutes attempting infant resuscitation, ninety seconds administering Pitocin to slow the mother's bleeding, eleven minutes redlining it to the Baptist Hospital where the mother was sutured, the child intubated, and my grandmother charged with practicing medicine without a license, a felony in the state of Alabama. A week later, when the baby died, they added involuntary manslaughter.

All of this was recorded in the court records she verified with her signature. She was in pretrial confinement. We visited her once on Independence Day and once on her birthday. My mother parked each time at a Payless close to the jailhouse, because she didn't want anyone seeing her van in the jailhouse lot. People would talk, she said. They did.

My grandmother was sentenced to five years in prison, suspended, and a three-year probation. After that, she couldn't get a job. Her income during probation came from sitting me Monday through Friday while my mother worked day shifts at the hospice center and accumulated evening credits toward her nursing degree. I was thirteen. I didn't need the sitting, but my grandmother needed the money.

My mother and grandmother didn't get along, so on Fridays my mother handed me eight twenty-dollar bills, which I ferried across the front porch to my grandmother, who sat at the table in her summer kitchen, smoking Pall Malls. "Count it," my grandmother said to me, and I counted by twenties, slapping the bills down onto the cedar planks of her table, feeling awfully important and afraid—of miscounting, of coming up short, of the woman at my right elbow and the woman at my back, either of whom might declare at any moment I was costing her too much.

My grandmother told me about the Cooper Hill midwives during those afternoons she kept me, skinning empty soda cans with her fish knife.

They were called "the Cooper Hill coven." A collection of midwives, of course, is not a coven. It's an expectation. The expectation of Cooper Hill was the last outpost of traditional midwifery in the state of Alabama.

Until August 1928, the midwives of Cooper Hill practiced as they had in the nineteenth century—no forceps, no ether, no twilight sleep. In Cooper Hill, when a woman was well into labor, she bid her eldest hang one bedsheet in the house window, and the news of her laboring slipped through the clay beds faster than the water of the Tennessee. One midwife came. Either Aunt Paulina or Carolina "Bama" Alder or Wanita or Rula Rousseau. Four Black women who attended the mothers of Cooper Hill at their lyings-in.

Sylvia joined them in the summer of 1928, leaving the city, where it was getting difficult for a midwife to find work. She rented Aunt Paulina's birthing house while Aunt Paulina completed her newfangled midwife training in Montgomery. I like to think they were friends—Sylvia and Aunt Paulina—at least as far as two women, one Black and one white, could have been friends in those days. Aunt Paulina trusted Sylvia enough to leave her to care for the birthing house. When Paulina returned from her training, they shared the space. For a time, they shared it amicably.

I like to think they slept, both of them, on the screened porch out back of the birthing house. They took turns on call each night, because a baby won't wait for sunup to crown. Whatever came later, I like to think they started as friends.

It changed, as circumstances do. One month after Aunt Paulina returned, jubilant, with her new Montgomery-school methods, there were no midwives in Cooper Hill. The expectation of Cooper Hill had been eliminated. Sylvia had vanished.

"What happened?" I'd ask my grandmother on our afternoons together. "What happened to the midwives?"

She'd spit out whatever was in her mouth (there was always something—chewing tobacco, fruit-flavored gum, ice cubes, toothpicks), and she'd say, "It was the day the doctors came."

Dr. Simpson: *We are making progress with regard to the midwife problem. Of the several thousand midwives in Alabama, hundreds already have been eliminated.*

Dr. Nicholson: *We cannot control the midwife, and we do not believe that the midwife can be entirely eliminated at present. All we are doing is carrying out a police supervision—there is no other word for it. The women are brought to account for any infraction of requirements. We have saved the lives of babies and mothers and improved obstetrics by our work. I believe that if we had a certain number of English-speaking, intelligent young women trained to care for women in labor, we would be able to get rid of a number of the mammies.*

Dr. Furman: *The day we arrived, the birthing house was jammed with men and women, some singing, some exhorting, and one fat "revrunt" was kneeling by a chair at the door praying and sweating fervently for the woman in labor to live. I commanded silence but without avail. Then I got provoked and grabbed the fat preacher by the collar with both hands and yanked him loose from that chair and out of the door. This decided action produced instant calm and I announced that as a doctor I was supported by the strong arm of the law and that I would indict the last mother's son of them if that room wasn't cleared of men instantly. Then the door and windows of that shack belched buck Negroes. One elderly mamma who seemed to be a special high priestess of the occasion opined that the patient was permeated with some sort of Divine Essence, though she didn't express it in exactly those words, and that it would be obviously sacrilegious to throw such obstacles as low-down common doctors' medicine in the way of the salvation of a human soul.*

"Sylvia was right there in Cooper Hill when the doctors arrived," my grandmother told me, cutting newspaper into strips to paper her cupboards.

August 29, 1928. The doctors came on horseback from the Children's Bureau "to inspect the midwives of St. Clair County at Cooper Hill for compliance with industry standards of cleanliness, equipment, and medical procedure."

The doctors forced the midwives from their birthing houses out into the street. A routine inspection. They took Aunt Paulina's leather bag and spilled it onto the gravel. Paulina had removed the glass bottles, stored them in a wooden chest in her birthing house. She'd replaced the bottles with sturdier spice jars and tobacco tins, in which she stored her new pharmaceuticals. She'd substituted newspaper for the linen lining, afraid of staining the white fabric with stool, afterbirth, or blood.

If newspaper lining and tobacco tins had been her only infractions, she might merely have been fined. But later that day, behind Paulina's birthing room, the doctors found a two-wheeled cart containing savin and tansy, rue and yarrow.

Aunt Paulina was charged with possessing illegal pharmaceuticals that could endanger an infant. She would later be sentenced to two years in Wetumpka Women's Penitentiary.

My grandmother heard the story from her father, who heard it from a nun, who heard it from a carpenter who saw it happen.

But what about Sylvia? Where was Sylvia Summer when Aunt Paulina was charged?

My grandmother lifted her hands, palms up. "That was the day Sylvia vanished."

Hundreds of Alabama midwives vanished in the twenties. To vanish might have meant any number of things. Murdered. Married. Brought up before the law. Crossed into Tennessee in the bed of a potato truck. Got a bit of land and kept to herself.

When my grandmother told me this story, I took Sylvia's vanishing to mean she, too, had been a victim of the day's proceedings. But then I read her letters.

The letters are addressed to Elizabeth Cromwell, who appears in a number of academic journals as a proponent of midwife education and women's rights. Sylvia Summer and Elizabeth Cromwell learned from the same Montgomery midwife in their teens. Their apprenticeships overlapped a year. In Elizabeth's earliest journal, Sylvia merits just a footnote, her name listed along with two others as "my fellows." This, I think, was discretion, not indifference. For years after, they stayed in touch.

Were they lovers? They had opportunity. They shared a room during their apprenticeship. Maybe they shared suppers of rice and black beans. Maybe, on cold nights, they shared a bed, lay whispering together. Elizabeth told Sylvia she'd make an excellent husband, an excellent father. Sylvia promised to build Elizabeth her own birthing house with a table and a sit-stool. They argued, of course. As lovers do. They fought about the importance of sterile birthing rooms. Elizabeth would have favored scrubbing and douching with chlorine. Sylvia, lye and cinnamon oil. Maybe such an argument caused them to part.

Elizabeth Cromwell eventually established nurse-midwife training programs in Montgomery. Her journal reads, "July 25, 1928—Walked five miles today to Hilton Head to graduate twelve midwives. After the graduation ceremony, the twelve mammies stood in a perfect line, magnificent in their starched caps and gowns, proudly offering their leather doctors' bags to the nurse for inspection. Inside, the equipment was well-ordered, sterilized, all they'd need to prepare a maternity bed."

This was Aunt Paulina's graduation ceremony.

August 2, 1928

Dearest Liz,

Paulina's just come from your school in Montgomery. She goes on about it, all high and mighty. I thought she'd stay in the city like the rest of your midwives, where there's a doctor on hand for every hiccup or milk-eye. I didn't expect your midwives in every corner of the state.

Paulina says she attended a Mrs. Beasley in Montgomery, who was my patient two years ago. She says there's hardly a woman in the city these days not attended by a doctor at her lying-in.

Some might read resentment here, a swelling bitterness. I read distress, the anxiety of a woman who chose a road she expected to follow for decades, then watched it dwindle to little more than a deer path.

Distress, as well, in the lines that follow—"Yesterday, Paulina and I attended a birth. The infant's shoulder wedged against the mother's pelvis, and Paulina said, *The doctor's on his way.* What doctor? There's not a doctor for thirty miles."

"You know, you're just like Sylvia," my grandmother often said. I loved to hear her say it. It was the nearest she or anyone came to complimenting me.

But *how* was I like Sylvia? I asked. At thirteen, I hoped to be X-rayed, dissected, revealed in that way to myself.

My grandmother smirked. "You're nosy," she said.

I was. "Where'd Sylvia go?" I always asked. "When she vanished?"

"Tennessee," said my grandmother.

"Really?"

Florida.

Down to the river to pray.

Next door.

Bottom of the deep blue sea.

My grandmother offered dozens of possibilities, but she always ended with this—"She was swallowed whole by that doctor's bag."

August 14, 1928

Dearest Liz,

Rula Rousseau died yesterday. She was headed up the hill to a birth. Hurrying, some trouble with the mother. Rousseau's heart gave out, most reckon. Paulina's locked herself away, grieving. She followed Rousseau as a girl, browned her linen, cooked her cords in the ashes for years.

Without Rousseau, the midwives will be hard-pressed to see to the needs of every woman. I might stay in Cooper Hill, though Paulina doesn't want me. There's no place for me in Montgomery. You know it as well as anyone. Here at least some women still choose my black haw over Paulina's aspirin. I only wish I could count one true friend among them.

Your Silver Spoon

P.S. I read that article you sent: "The mammies' nails are dirty, their hands indescribable." Tell me, Elizabeth, were those my indescribable hands?

The doctor's bag caught Sylvia Summer by her skirt. It spun her around, tossed her into the air, and stretched open as she plummeted. It nearly split, attempting to accommodate the considerable breadth of Sylvia's shoulders. Sylvia Summer made no sound as the bag swallowed her. The bag snapped shut. A tiny red tongue flicked once around the handle to polish it, then the tongue disappeared as well.

"That's ridiculous. You made it up." At thirteen, I had no patience for fantasy.

"I didn't."

"How could you know that?"

The doctors saw it. The midwives watched it happen. The townspeople had gathered. They saw it. They still talk about it. They say Aunt Paulina rushed to open the bag after, but there was nothing inside save the newspaper lining. One of the doctors picked up the bag and carried it away.

"You don't know she was eaten. Sylvia might've jumped into the bag. She might've been trying to escape the doctors."

"Those doctors weren't after Sylvia." My grandmother turned her head and blew smoke just past my left ear. "Besides, she left her cart."

"Her cart?"

My grandmother studied me. "You're a whore," she said, delighted. She leaned her chair back on two legs, kicking her feet up onto the table. "What wouldn't you do for a story? I might tell you to lick the wax from my ear, you'd do it." She loved to find these little flaws, desires, any hold she might have over me.

She wanted to impress me. I was, that year, her only company, her only regular audience. This, I think, was the reason for her fantasies. The women in my family have always been capable of invention.

"What do you mean, she left her cart?"

Then that third letter.

August 23, 1928

Elizabeth,

Paulina's insufferable. Last week, she snuffed the candle Missouria had lit beneath the birthing bed. The mother wasn't more than twenty. Her first delivery, and Paulina starts an argument in the birthing room. She's lost us more than one patient. Women are traveling to Gadsden for their deliveries, and I don't blame them.

I've tried telling Paulina the women here want a birthing candle, want to cook the cord. Paulina won't hear it. The doctor's techniques plus mine, she says, and I'm twice as sure of success.

You'd say she's right. You think you know better than the rest of us, but when she's up against the grindstone, Paulina's not so different than I am. Yesterday, she restored the menses of a girl thin-hipped and young, who had no reason to bring her baby to term. Paulina closed me out of the birthing room, but she let

Wanita stay. Wanita told me Paulina fixed that girl with savin twice boiled and strained through a cloth. Just as I'd have done.

You might not have such a handle on your nurses, Elizabeth, as you believe. At the end of the day, however you dress her up, Paulina's a granny, same as I am.

Sylvia

Six days after Sylvia Summer posted this last letter, the doctors arrived in Cooper Hill.

It's possible their coming had nothing to do with Sylvia's letters. Perhaps the inspection was already scheduled. But I think the doctors came because of her. Elizabeth Cromwell couldn't afford to have her trained midwives performing abortions, especially not herbal abortions. Sylvia knew that. Sylvia planned it all.

I was twenty when I finally read these letters, five years after my grandmother's probation ended. The Alabama Department of Health had made them public, part of a national campaign to improve transparency within the organization and "come to terms with the racial injustices of our past."

I took the letters immediately to my grandmother. It had been three years since I'd seen her. She'd invited me over a few times—for dinner on a Thursday, for Sunday brunch. I was always busy. I was choreographing a ribbon dance with the color guard or traveling with the French horns to Tallahassee.

"Letters from Sylvia," she said when I arrived. "That's a treat."

She'd set a table in her summer kitchen with potatoes and pinto beans and succotash, and she insisted we eat before reading the letters. I ate little, because she'd creamed her potatoes with mayonnaise and cooked the beans in, of all things, lard.

"My eyes aren't what they used to be," she said when I attempted to foist the letters on her. "You'll have to read them to me."

I did. I read without stopping, without looking up from the page to gauge her reaction. When I'd finished, I asked—in the clipped, unemotional tone with which a young journalist deals a violent but necessary blow—"What did Sylvia carry in her cart?"

A pause.

Drop-daisy. Oil of cloves. Pennyroyal. Savin.

Savin?

Certainly. Savin.

But savin was illegal. Savin caused abortion. Abortion was illegal.

Any midwife worth her salt kept savin on hand.

Did she have savin in her cart on Cooper Hill? Was it her cart they found in back of Aunt Paulina's house? Was it her cart that got Aunt Paulina arrested? Was it her fault?

Was it vicious, my grandmother's grin? Maybe. Maybe a little vicious. The savage smile of a woman who knows something you should have figured out by now. Since you haven't, she must tell you, must pull the caul back from the wrinkled, ugly newborn. "It might have been. It could have been. I never said she was good."

Sitting there in front of my grandmother, I felt not disappointment, not betrayal, but a heady sense of importance—one of those rare moments whose significance is realized not in retrospect but right there, in the moment itself. My grandmother sponged the last juice from her plate with a puff-roll, appearing utterly at ease, unaware that the foundations of the world had shaken and rearranged themselves.

"She framed Paulina. She knew Paulina would be the one they went after."

"Oh, she wasn't after Paulina. Sylvia was after Elizabeth."

"She was awful. She was racist."

"No more than normal." My grandmother spooned the last of the beans directly from the serving dish into her mouth and said, mouth full, "I know you admired Sylvia. Something of a hero for you."

"She never was," I said. "For you, maybe."

"You loved those stories. You'd always ask me for those stories."

"I never asked." And if I had, what of it. I was thirteen. "The story you told me was never the real story anyway."

"Sure it was."

"In your story Sylvia's a victim."

"I never said she was a victim."

"She gets swallowed up."

"That's not the end. You never let me get to the end."

After Sylvia disappeared into the doctor's bag, Paulina pried it open. She reached down into the depths of the bag. She got hold of something heavy within that bag, or something heavy got hold of her. She braced herself. She pulled. She worked her torso back and forth like you'd work a seized bolt with a ratchet. For a moment, Sylvia's forehead was visible, crowning, at the mouth of the bag. Sylvia's voice issued up from inside the bag saying, "Come with me, Paulina," saying, "Let go of me." Paulina didn't let go. She got hold of Sylvia's apron and pulled. But Sylvia fought. Sylvia dug down into the folds of the bag like a tick into its mound. Sylvia thrashed until her apron tore. She got away. Paulina fell back from the bag with nothing in her hand but the bib off that apron. No other evidence Sylvia had been there at all.

"I don't see what that's supposed to mean."

"It's not supposed to *mean* anything."

"You're saying it wasn't the doctors. It was just the two of them in the end, fighting each other."

"Who says they were fighting? Maybe Paulina was trying to save Sylvia from that bag. Maybe Sylvia was telling Paulina to come with her, so she'd be safe from the doctors."

"Sylvia was the one who called the doctors. She sold Aunt Paulina out."

"We don't know that."

"We know Sylvia wasn't trying to save anybody but herself. You run away from something that way, it's always about protecting your own hide."

"Maybe you're right." My grandmother smiled a smile that says you've lost and lost badly. You've argued your way into a corner, and she's so polite, so generous she won't even point out how. "Maybe that's true." She lit a cigarette, lit one for me without asking if I smoked. I didn't, not regularly, but I did with her that afternoon. "You remember the day I was arrested?" she asked.

Of course I remembered. I'd watched from my mother's mini-van, parked in the lot of the Baptist Hospital. My mother cracked the windows of the minivan and told me, "You stay right here." I watched my grandmother attempt to climb into the police cruiser with her hands cuffed behind her. She couldn't, so they took away the cuffs, let her use her hands to pull herself up into the shotgun seat. I watched her settle her purse on the dash and mouth instructions to my mother through the window as the cruiser pulled away. It was easy, on that day, to imagine she was leaving in a cab to spend a few weeks at the bay, as she often did in summer.

"I saved the mother's life that day," she said to me. This I hadn't heard. "The doctor told me when we arrived at the hospital. He said giving her the Pitocin right away like I did saved her life."

My grandmother called all doctors shysters and quacks. She refused to stand in the same room with them. She refused to attend my birth, because my mother chose to deliver in a hospital.

"The doctor said it," she repeated, as if his being a doctor added legitimacy to his words.

It would be years before I wrote an essay—"Why My Grandma's a Felon"—about her case and the long history of Alabama's anti-midwife legislation, so long I would forget this moment, forget the way her words lifted and restored me. She'd revealed herself, her hypocrisy. All along, she'd wanted the approval of the doctors, a power she claimed to disdain. Like Sylvia, courting Elizabeth. I wasn't like either one of them. I had words for what they were—small-minded, selfish. With those words, I put myself up on a platform they couldn't reach and would never reach. I was safe there—from her and from Sylvia and from anything their lives might suggest about my own. This was the moment when writing the essay became possible.

"Don't be a stranger," my grandmother said to me later that night, as she packed potatoes and succotash into a Tupperware for me to take home. "You're like Sylvia, liable to disappear on me."

I understood, then, why she'd grinned when I blamed Sylvia for running away. She thought I, too, was the type to flee, to distance myself from trouble, let someone else take the fall. The unfairness of this, from a woman I'd sat with every afternoon of her probation, stung.

"I'm not going anywhere," I said, and I kissed her cheek and got out of there.

One month before my grandmother's death, my mother called me. I was living in Oregon, writing copy for an ad agency.

"She's been asking why you never come to see her," my mother said. "Seeing as how those afternoons you spent together were so rich."

I was silent. I didn't understand.

"In your essay," she said. "You wrote how rich they were."

Had I written that? Had I used that word, *rich*? I suppose I had. I must've. I didn't remember. I'd published the essay five years before and hadn't read it since. I had no intention of reading it again. It seemed the work of an altogether different person, and I resented my mother holding me responsible for it.

"She called me after it came out. She was peeved."

"I defended her midwifery. I'd expect her to be flattered."

"You said her admiration for Sylvia was prejudiced."

"It *is* prejudiced."

"But you didn't have to put that in the essay. You didn't have to write an essay at all."

"I needed to apologize for Sylvia. Someone had to apologize for Sylvia."

"You can't apologize for Sylvia. You want to apologize to somebody, you can tell your grandmother you're sorry for making her out like you did, making her out to be a bigot just to show how progressive you are."

"It's not like that. It's not one of us against the other."

"There's not one line in that essay about you admiring Sylvia, too."

I never did visit my grandmother. She'd have wanted to set things straight about Sylvia. "You're like Sylvia," she would say, and I would have to defend myself.

My grandmother died of an ingrown toenail, an infection any course of antibiotics would have cleared in a week. I felt a certain satisfaction hearing from my mother how she'd packed the toe with willow bark and boneset.

You expect certain things of a woman like that.

In 1933, as part of the Federal Writers Project, Aunt Paulina, "one of the last practicing granny midwives," was interviewed by an oral historian from the University of Tennessee.

PAULINA: I never did want to be a midwife. The Lord told me I was to be a midwife, and I told Him, "No, thank you." I saw what Miss Rula Rousseau went through, up all hours of the night, traveling. And I mean traveling. We would go out at night . . . It was horse, buggy, mule or buggy, or wagon, and I rode in all of them at night, going through the waters, snow and ice.

But He said, "Well, that's what you're going to be."

Everywhere I went after that babies would fall out of their mothers, fall right in front of me, and I didn't have a choice but to catch them. It was catch them or let them drop onto the floor. They started calling me a midwife. I couldn't stop them doing it.

INTERVIEWER: But you were trained as a midwife?

PAULINA: I met a doctor who told me I could train at no cost to myself. I trained at the Montgomery School. We followed the doctors. We went around with them, helped with the setting up and the cleaning up. Sometimes we delivered the baby ourselves, because the doctor was late getting to the birthing room. We had these leather bags to take around with us—nice bags with glass bottles right inside for the medicine.

INTERVIEWER: You were arrested. When was that? Do you remember that day?

PAULINA: The day? The day wasn't interesting. Other people, maybe, were interested in the doctors. I'd seen enough doctors by that point to be sick of them. There was one doctor, after it was all over, he picked up my doctor's bag and polished the handle with his shirtsleeve. I remember that, because it's something I'd have liked to do.

SURROGATE

—

On Thursday after their Kegels, while the surrogates drink ginger shots and lie belly down on bolsters, Brighten declares that she trusts her husband.

"Oh, honey," Jamila says, rolling her bolster to crack her spine.

Mona swallows her ginger shot. "You trust him to do what, exactly?"

"Just generally."

"I don't see what could bring you to that," Mona says. Brighten expects this from Mona, an ex-gymnast, head to toe tattoos. But the other four surrogates are also smiling and glancing away, as if she is stupid, naïve. She looks to Doc for understanding, but Doc is measuring Lane's abdomen, paying no attention to Brighten.

"It was because of the fire," Brighten explains. The Sandy Creek Fire, which had blackened the Kansas prairie nine years before. She remembers the day exactly. She can explain.

Brighten saw that fire from the Starlite Drive-in. She was fifteen, Orson a year older. He'd taken her to see an oldie—*The*

Towering Inferno—on the big screen. They'd been dating just a few months at that point. Six years later, they would marry.

The drive from Bentonville was five hours. Brighten kept her window down. Orson's was taped over, so it didn't open. They dialed between the two stations on the radio—one Christian, one rez. They couldn't hear either over the wind. Brighten combed her hair with her fingers, and the shed hair whipped in circles around the car.

There were drive-ins in Arkansas, but they hadn't considered those. The point was to spend a night west of the border. It was her first time out of the state. Orson's, too.

The teller at the ticket window said, "You'd do better to get out of here. Fire's too close for comfort."

Orson refused. They'd come five hours to see the movie, and they'd see it.

"I'm out soon as I press play. It's just the two of you," the teller said.

But when they pulled into the movie lot, they saw another car parked close to the screen. This reassured them. They decided to stay as long as the other car stayed.

The drive-in screen was three times the length of a man across and nearly twice as tall. The faces—the faces were huge. Brighten could have bouldered across Paul Newman's nose, dug her fingers into his tear duct and hung from it. She kept forgetting it wasn't real. She imagined the screen itself must be hot as the burning San Francisco tower. The smoke thick in her lungs was surely California smoke. She expected the screen to go up in a sheath of flame as the Glass Tower had, expected sparks to leap from the aluminum into the surrounding hayfields, fenced in barbed wire to keep kids from sneaking in on foot.

Of course, it wasn't the screen on fire. It was the prairie grass two counties away—fire in the cattle fields, fire in Sandy Creek valley, the creek itself aflame. Sitting in the car, she watched the fire crawl along her horizon line, a small red-glowing worm. Twice, she and Orson considered leaving. But the other car stayed.

"You think they've got soda?" Brighten asked, nodding to the car. They'd finished a two-liter of 7-Up, and she could feel her tongue dry and swollen against her teeth.

"I don't know," Orson said. He watched the screen, where a woman opened the stairwell door to a wall of smoke.

"Want to ask them?"

They went together across the empty parking spaces. They wanted to know how long the family was planning to stay. They wanted to talk to someone.

They approached the driver's window, prepared to knock politely.

The car was empty. Just a crushed pack of Camels by the brake pedal and two tampons in the groove of the side seat. Deserted.

Brighten slapped her palm against the windshield. Orson kicked the tire. Brighten tried the door handles.

But the knocking, when it came, came from the trunk.

"Sorry?" This is Mona, who is digging one elbow into the space between Jamila's shoulder blades.

Something in the trunk knocked. A tapping in response to their noise.

Something in the trunk said, "Is someone there?"

❦

Brighten used to love Thursdays. All week, she looked forward to Thursdays. She looked forward, stubbornly, to leaving her daughter, Roo, with Orson's sister for the day. She looked forward, privately, to the company of Doc Lacher and the surrogates. She loved the drive to Doc's homestead—forty minutes alone through pasture grazed down to buttercups and pigweed. She was calm on those drives. Perfectly focused. She tuned in to her body. When she'd carried Roo, she was tuned to Roo—the weight, the movement, the presence. It's different as a surrogate. She cares about the health of the fetus, but not the person of it. She doesn't love it. It's her body she loves—the accommodation of her muscles. She looks forward to the third trimester—the swollen ankles, the stretch marks, the distension of her abdomen, the physical marks of her capacity, her endurance. She will be gentle with herself in late pregnancy, as she used to be after a day of climbing—massaging her white and bloodless toes, taping her blistered fingers. She wants a reason to be gentle.

Doc taught her to tune in to her body this way. Doc Lacher. Her surrogacy agent. Her coach. Her friend. Yes, still her friend.

Brighten discovered Doc Lacher on television. An interview special from KFSM out of Fayetteville. Four o'clock news. Brighten had been watching coverage of a murder that took place just ten minutes by car from her double-wide. The accused was a thirty-one-year-old woman. She'd suffocated her neighbor with a pincushion, put the body in the bottom drawer of a chiffonier, and dropped the chiffonier off at a Salvation Army Donation

Center. The woman accused had been unable to conceive, and the newscaster suggested she'd killed her neighbor because she wanted the child her neighbor cared for, a little blond girl whose picture they showed when they weren't showing the courthouse.

"Liar," Brighten said to the thirteen-inch television balanced on top of their microwave. She sipped water from a coffee mug and rubbed a square of cinnamon crunch cereal between her fingers to scrub it of excess sugar. She handed the scrubbed square to two-year-old Roo, who was opening and closing cabinets. Roo put the square in her mouth to wet it, then stuck it to the cabinet door.

Brighten believed the woman was guilty, but she didn't believe the woman wanted the child. It was too easy. Too deliberate. Brighten didn't think the murder was anything the woman had planned. It was a spontaneous act. Caused by the sun, which baked the metal of the woman's mobile home, or by the shitty front door hanging off its hinges again, or by the anthill sprung up in the yard she'd just spent a fortune treating for pests. Maybe the woman went to borrow some grounds from her neighbor, and the old woman said, "Get your fat ass off my lawn," or threw a handful of dandelions gone to seed over the property line. On a hot day or a Tuesday, it wouldn't take more than that.

They brought Doc Lacher on the news to discuss rising infertility rates. Every county in Arkansas had seen rates go up. The Big Lots in Fayetteville had started stocking little jars of Ova-Boost and FertilAid.

"It's a good year to be a surrogate," Doc said.

The papers blamed infertility on women who smoked, drank too much liquor and Mountain Dew; they blamed diabetes, blamed girls too young to be messing around, boys subsisting on hot dogs and meth, boys who can't shoot, can't swim.

Doc Lacher blamed the water. "Don't drink it," Doc said on the television that day. Don't let your dog drink it. Don't bathe any child under two in it. Keep it out of your eyes. Keep it away from your succulents.

Brighten set down the glass from which she'd been sipping, watched the television screen through the liquid blur. Brighten had heard stories of reservoirs gone bad, of kids who were late to talking, because they drank down lead. But she'd never worried about the water she, Orson, and Roo drank from their sand-point well.

It'll take the finish off a nonstick pan.

It'll dissolve your corneas.

It'll wither your ovaries.

"Let's talk about your surrogates," the newscaster prompted.

"I don't have surrogates," Doc Lacher said. "I have athletes, and you should see the babies my girls produce."

Brighten leaned toward the television. She was an athlete. She'd spent weekends in high school driving east to Red Rock Point, climbed every face of the sandstone outcropping first with ropes, then without. She got a partial scholarship to Arkansas State for speed climbing, was the first woman from the region to make the Olympic prequalifiers. There, she hit a loose hold. She fell and was disqualified. She'd planned to try again the next year, but the next year she was pregnant with Roo. The year after she was tired like she'd never been tired. The year after that, she'd lost it—whatever it was—the drive, the fire, the arrogance that can lead a woman to bank everything on a toehold and fingers dusted with chalk.

"Do you miss it?" Orson sometimes asked.

"Of course," she answered, and she withstood the strum of hope, her belief that he had some plan—a trip to Red Rock or an indoor wall or maybe a nanny. She withstood the disappointment that followed when he nodded twice and ducked into the kitchen for a beer, as if the question and some accompanying sympathy were all he could offer, all he was required to offer.

At the bottom of the TV screen, the news ticker said what it took to be a surrogate: *Between 25 and 35 years of age. One healthy child, naturally delivered. Doesn't smoke. Doesn't drink. No dietary restrictions. Exercises regularly.*

Brighten dipped one finger absently into her glass and let Roo nurse the moisture from it. Brighten fit the description for a surrogate.

There was a time when Brighten fit descriptions for outdoor action shoots (shoulders that bunched when she tensed them) and toothpaste commercials (whitened with strips). That time had passed, but she still had the body. A muscular body, used to chimneying and one-finger pull-ups. Thicker around the middle, sure, but it was still strong.

Brighten pulverized a cinnamon square, let the pieces drop to the ground. *It's a good year to be a surrogate.*

The consultation with Doc was free of charge. No commitment, except a sixteen-mile drive to the address listed on the website.

Doc herself answered the door. No waiting room, no receptionist, just Doc in Dickies coveralls with a stud in one ear and a clutch of hair beneath her chin. Black, wiry hair, which Brighten wanted—surprisingly, frighteningly—to touch.

"Perfect," Doc said when she'd finished measuring Brighten's vitals, her maximum heart rate and oxygen consumption. "You'll be perfect."

The evening after the consultation, Brighten picked Orson up at the frac pond, where he hauled water for Southwestern. Four hundred gallons of water to every well, six hundred gallons away. Away, that easy blind word. Away is a gravel pit not an hour from Fayetteville. Take Highway 16 west out of town, make a right on the forest roads, you can get away, too.

"I'm going to be a surrogate," she told him, setting Roo down to play in the gravel beside the pond.

"A surrogate what?" he said.

Orson hadn't always hauled water. In high school, in the time after their trip to the drive-in, he talked about being a film professor. He didn't stick to that, didn't stick to anything. When they married, he was part-time at Arkansas State, driving over-the-road to pay tuition and making progress toward a degree in world languages. Sometimes he'd still say funny things—call wind farms *quick saw dick*. When he said things like that, she'd feel herself pull away from him, a reaction she couldn't help.

After she had Roo, Orson started driving local, which meant he made less and was around more. She used to give him a hard time—"False advertising, that person you were when I married you"—but it went nowhere with Orson, saying things like that.

She liked to drive out to the frac pond with Roo asleep in the
back seat and meet Orson at the gates fringed with barbed wire,
liked to have him buzz her car inside, to hear the gates wheel
closed behind her. The security added some gravity, some importance to his work. It was easier at the frac ponds, there beside his
pup-and-truck, to be proud of him.

"A surrogate for a kid. To carry a kid," she said. "I'm perfect
for it."

"You mean for money?"

"Fifty grand, plus expenses."

Behind him, aerators threw dirty water up into the sun. Roo
reached with her hands to touch the spray. Brighten didn't mind
if Roo touched it, but Orson wouldn't allow it. This was another
thing she liked about the frac ponds—they were dangerous, a
danger from which Orson could protect them. She set him up, in
little ways like this, to impress her.

"We have money," Orson said.

"I want to go back to school," she said. There wasn't that kind
of money.

"We'll find the money."

Like they'd misplaced it. Like it was bundled at the back of
their sock drawer. "It's not about the money."

Orson had proposed at the frac pond, sat her up high beside
him in his pup-and-truck and pulled out a plastic ring he'd se-
creted away in the ashtray. After she agreed to marry him, he
walked her down to the pond and flicked his Bic lighter, touched
the flame to the water's surface.

Once, nothing.

Twice, nothing.

On his third try, a blush of fire. It skittered across the water and was gone.

Methane, he said. They were surrounded by it. In the shale, in the river. Every bit of this land will light. That was Orson's idea of ceremony.

"You can do something else," he said now. "Some other work."

"What other work?"

"It's hard on the body, pregnancy."

"Oh, is it? I hadn't noticed."

Not what she meant. Not what she wanted—the flash of snark, of bitterness pure and hard. A signal, inviting him to face off against her in the quick-paced arguments that traversed always the same terrain. His chronic lateness. Her come-and-go depression. His weight. Her gluten intolerance.

He shook his head. "I wasn't saying you hadn't noticed."

"I want to be pregnant again."

Brighten had liked being pregnant. She was good at it. Talented. Carrying Roo, she slept better. Ate better. She never felt nauseous, never felt the frightening impulses—taking scissors to her belly, drowning herself in a community pool—other women discussed.

Mothering was something else. In the months after Roo was born, she often imagined binding Roo's small limbs to the trunk of her body and reinserting her. She still had the extra space, extra skin. She could carry Roo until Roo was larger, easier, both of them better prepared.

"If you want another kid, we can have another kid."

"I don't want another kid."

Orson wrapped his arm around Roo to prevent her dunking her head into the pond. "A well can be fracked three times," he said, "before it's depleted."

"I don't know what you're trying to say."

"I'd rather you did something else."

She'd decided. At some point in the course of the conversation, she'd decided to do it. It had become less a physical thing, less about the fact of a blastocyst, the fact of her body carrying a fetus, and more about having something in her life, some center. Failing to do it would not be like failing to finish an intimidating climb, but like failing to secure the toprope anchor on which her life depended.

Each surrogate had her reason. Mona carried for gay couples, said it was her way of making a difference. Jamila carried first for her sister, liked the intimacy of it, liked the way her mailbox at Christmas filled with photos of kids from Florida and Ontario. Her husband bought her prenatal massages and injected her with hormones during the crucial, early months. Lane was paying her way through grad school, but she got lunch weekly with the intended parents and wanted the kid to call her Aunty. Brighten had no interest in keeping in touch with the kid. She was the only one who didn't want to see the kid again, the only one whose husband refused to accompany her to meetings with the intended parents. "I don't want to meet them," he said. "I'm not part of this."

This was new for Brighten. Before this, whatever Brighten had done, Orson had been a part of it.

At the drive-in that night, Orson and Brighten had determined it was a woman in the trunk. They determined this from the timbre of her voice and because a woman was more likely than a man to find herself locked in a trunk. The woman in the trunk said to them, "You'll have to help me." Relief in her tone. As if, merely by being discovered, she'd been saved.

"How'd you get in there?" Orson asked.

"How near is the fire?" said the woman.

"Did something happen to you?" Brighten asked.

"How near is the fire?" said the woman.

"Did someone lock you in?"

"You have to go and get someone," the woman said. "One of you has to go. Get the attendant."

"He's gone," Orson said. "I guess everybody but us is gone."

"You have a car?"

They determined, by silent agreement, not to answer this.

"Is there a key?" Orson asked.

"There's no key."

"Or a crowbar. Or an ax. We could break the window."

"There's no ax."

"We'll find something. There must be something. We'll go and look."

"Don't go. Not both of you. One of you stay."

They ignored this, distrusting the woman's attempt to separate them. They both went looking. For a coat hanger. For a tire iron. Brighten walked the perimeter of the lot looking for a rock the size of her fist.

They found an old orange and a plastic toilet lid. They told the woman in the trunk, "We can't find anything else."

"I need you to get an adult," said the woman. "One of you go find someone, and one of you stay here with me."

Orson and Brighten looked at each other. "No," Orson said, and Brighten felt a thrill at his daring, his refusal to obey.

"We don't want to do that," Brighten said.

"We're together," Orson said, and Brighten nodded. The word had never felt so appropriate, as if she and Orson were the only people left in the state. The woman in the trunk, too, of course, but Brighten put her in a different category—she was clearly alone.

"You have to get someone," said the woman in the trunk. "Is the fire very close?"

Orson and Brighten didn't respond. They didn't want to think about the fire. They turned their attention to the screen, where Susan Flannery and her lover burned to two delicate crisps in each other's arms.

"Are you there?" the woman called through the seam of the trunk. "Are you still there?" She sounded sorry for whatever she might have said to offend them.

It was in that moment Brighten first determined she could trust Orson. On the screen, men repelled down elevator shafts.

Men attempted helicopter rescues. Orson put one hand on the trunk of the car, tapped once, let the woman know he was there. Nothing drastic. Nothing dangerous. Nothing heroic. Orson wasn't a man to go to extremes.

Now, Brighten dreads Thursdays. She drives slowly on the washboard roads, squeezing her thighs before inching over potholes to ensure nothing jostles her cervix. She circles Doc's property until she is five minutes late, ten, considers simply driving back to the city, making up some excuse—Roo has an ear infection, she won't stop screaming, Orson's sister has colon cancer, Orson's sister can't keep Roo. But Doc would know. Doc would know Brighten was avoiding the surrogates, avoiding Doc. Last Thursday, just before making the inevitable turn up the gravel drive, Brighten leaned forward, closed her eyes, and bit hard into the rubber of the steering wheel. A piece came away in her mouth, and she swallowed it.

Her hands tremble sometimes, as she climbs from her car. She expects to faint. She doesn't faint. She can no longer predict the patterns and impulses of her body.

She discovered this two weeks ago, when Doc kept her back after class to discuss her health and the health of the fetus. Her most recent blood work was concerning. Heavy, Doc said. Her blood was heavy. Thick with sticky hydrocarbons and wheeling benzenes. There was a danger of premature birth. Because the environment was toxic to the fetus, the fetus might try to exit that environment prematurely.

"Heavy?" Brighten sat on the floor, arms wrapped around a foam triangle. Why hadn't she anticipated this? *Heavy* was a word from the centrifuge, but Brighten understood it at once. Her eyelids were heavy. Her limbs were heavy. Her placenta was heavy—a good, anchoring heaviness. Her blood—why had she never considered her blood?

Doc asked her questions—Had Brighten drunk anything? Smoked anything? Of course not. Not even coffee? Soda? No. Eaten any shellfish? Any ethnic foods? Any artificial sweeteners? Any soft cheeses? Any shark, swordfish, snails? Changed the dosage of any drugs? Sniffed paint thinner? Had she considered hurting herself? Killing herself? Brighten shook her head, shook her head, felt she was somehow making it worse for herself by saying no, no, no, as if she were declining an offer Doc, in her generosity, was making, a bargain, a plea deal.

She wanted Doc Lacher to say it wasn't her fault, that there was nothing she could have done, but she couldn't ask for this. The doctor acted different now than she had before—impersonal, professional. "Are you feverish or just distressed?" she asked when she noticed the sweat Brighten left on the foam. She thumbed Brighten's lymph nodes. "Distressed. That won't help anything."

Brighten was not in love with Doc Lacher. She was certain of this, because she often had to convince Orson of it. When acquaintances at a potluck had once offered Orson their congratulations, he shook his head. "Pregnant by her mistress," he'd said, and she blushed and excused herself to the kitchen, where she filled a glass with tap water, then poured it down the drain. She found a twenty-four-pack of spring water. She drank one bottle right there and slipped two more into her shoulder bag. In her surrogacy agreement, Brighten had agreed to drink only bottled water, but at home she still drank from the tap. She couldn't see her way to paying seven dollars for a week's worth of water. She'd grown up okay, after all, and she'd been drinking groundwater all her life.

In bed that night, Brighten said to Orson, "Don't call her my mistress. It's not an affair." Roo slept between them. She'd refused to go down for the sitter, and Brighten had refused to spend an hour putting her down when they returned.

"You'd rather be there," Orson said. "I can see it, I can tell. Over me, over your own daughter, you'd rather be with the surrogates. With Doc, a woman who wouldn't look twice at you if you couldn't carry a baby."

"I don't care about them more than Roo," Brighten said, her hands over Roo's ears. "Doc worries about us, that's all. She takes care of us. We have a connection."

"A connection. Great. Good for you."

How could Brighten explain Doc so Orson would understand? Doc slept with a Colt revolver on the memory foam pillow where her husband—may he rest in peace—had once laid his sweet head. She had twenty beef cattle on a homestead that bordered the Ozark forest. She'd built that homestead—not with her own hands, but with her own money. She had opinions and wasn't shy about sharing them. "Ozark boys these days don't know anything but fracking," she'd say. "If they could, they'd frack in the roads and the bathrooms and the goddamn Marriott, frack all day, break for a cheeseburger, frack through the night. I caught a pair last week trying to frack in my front yard, ran them off with my garden hose." ("That's me she's talking about," Orson said. "Not you," Brighten said. "You're not like that.") Doc had enemies. She'd received newspaper photos of herself with her eyes inked out and a narrow beard scribbled in pen across her chin. She'd received letters—*You're a pimp. A profiteer. You prey on dreams of parenthood.* Someone had tried to poison her cattle with arsenic, but the poisoner had dropped the d-CON wrapper near the feed bin, and Doc saw it, and she threw out all that feed. ("Sounds paranoid," Orson said. "She's tough," Brighten countered. "She's dealt with a lot of shit.") Doc had never lost a baby or a surrogate. The breech cases, the partial occlusions, the preemies, the one with gestational diabetes, Doc freed and stabilized them all.

Brighten had been Doc's favorite. She knew this. In Brighten's first interview with the parents-to-be, Doc had said, "If I were choosing a surrogate, I'd choose Brighten." Perhaps she said that every time, but Brighten didn't think so. Later, at twenty-eight weeks, Brighten predicted she needed a stitch in her cervix, and she did need one. "No one knows her body like Brighten knows her body," Doc said to the surrogates that Thursday, and Brighten felt elated, all out of proportion to the compliment.

Confronted by her heavy blood, Brighten had said to Doc, "I'm sorry." Brighten had the sort of headache that starts in one temple and pulses down the spine. She believed this was the sensation of remembering, of drilling back through every action, every meal of the past six months, trying to understand what she had missed, how she had fallen out of step with her body. Mining exhausts the deposit. She was exhausted.

"Your health is my health," Doc said.

After their Kegels, while the surrogates drink ginger shots and lie belly down on bolsters, Doc tells them about Brighten's blood. Each has her theory.

Jamila says, "You been drinking? Alcohol? Caffeine?"

"Or the water," Doc adds. "Have you been drinking tap water?"

Brighten is saved from responding by Mona. "It's your husband," Mona says. "Poisoning you."

"It's not Orson. Orson doesn't cook."

"Wouldn't have to be his cooking," Doc says. "Could be in your tea. Could be in your soap."

"There was a woman I read about," Mona said, "whose husband had been lacing her blueberry cheesecake with arsenic for years."

"That's sweet," says Jamila with a lazy cat smile, resting her head against the mound of Mona's belly.

Brighten nearly says Orson doesn't do those things, doesn't make her tea or cheesecake, doesn't splurge on fancy liquid soap. Brighten and Orson both use unscented bar soap with nothing added. No poison, no oils, not even any moisturizer. But Brighten can't be sure whether this is an argument for Orson or against him, so she says nothing.

Orson and Brighten hadn't taken advantage of the woman in the trunk. They hadn't asked her for anything. They could have taken advantage. The woman in the trunk offered them things. She offered Brighten a pair of black ballet shoes.

"I don't dance," Brighten said.

"She can't," Orson said. "It's something with her ankles."

"Don't," Brighten said to Orson. Brighten had too-short tendons, which caused her to walk on her toes, made dancing an embarrassment. She wore cowboy boots with heels, so it wasn't noticeable. Only Orson and her family knew—and now this woman, this stranger. "Shut up."

Orson only shrugged. "What's it matter?" he said. Brighten understood then what Orson had understood. They could say anything at all to the woman in the trunk. She wouldn't tell anyone. She couldn't tell anyone unless they somehow let her out.

The woman in the trunk said, "They can fix your ankles."

Brighten knew they could fix them. In Fayetteville, they'd have fixed her with leg casts or a slice through her Achilles before she started school. But an hour east of the city, some things were overlooked and some things were left too long and you lived with them.

"I could find you someone to fix that if you get me out," said the woman in the trunk.

"I don't mind it," Brighten said.

"What about the other one?" the woman asked. "The boy. What could I do for you?"

Orson thought. Orson put one hand on his forehead and kneaded the skin there. Orson turned to Brighten, shrugged his shoulders, mouthed, "Help me." Brighten returns sometimes to this moment. It's a moment she's fond of—Orson thrown not by a woman trapped in a trunk but by that woman offering him a gift.

Brighten said, "He'd like an implant for his upper incisor."

Orson's tongue went to the gap in his teeth. He didn't contradict her. "She'd like a haircut," he said.

"He'd like a beard."

"She'd like a nose piercing." This was true, though she'd never mentioned it to him. Brighten nodded, impressed.

"He'd like to live somewhere he doesn't speak the language."

"She'd like a slab a thousand feet high."

They inched forward, naming each other, finding, to their surprise, that they knew the other well. "He'd like to wear a dress with sequins."

"She'd like to make more money than her dad makes."

"He'd like to drive west tonight and never come back." On the screen, the windows of the Glass Tower exploded outward, crumbs of glass falling to the street below.

In the drive-in lot, the fire appeared to be thickening. The glowworm on the horizon had swelled into an arc of light, competing with the glow from the screen. The smoke was thicker, too, making Orson's voice sound raspy, adult, as he said, "She'd like to make out right now in the back seat of your car."

Brighten has tried, in the years of their marriage, to restart this conversation. It always dissolves into teasing—he'd like a soda dispenser in the kitchen, she'd like a job you can do in your pajamas. Whatever clarity they had that day was fleeting—the result maybe of the woman listening, or of the fire, or of all they had yet to learn about each other.

"I have an idea," the woman said. "For the boy. Come close, I'll tell you. Come close." She tapped to show him where to come. Orson went to the trunk, put his ear against the metal. He listened, breathless, to whatever the woman promised him.

"How's that?" the woman said.

"Okay," Orson said.

"Go and get someone, then," the woman said. "Go and get an adult. Both of you."

Given her blessing, they went. Together. They left in Orson's car and never returned and never told anyone about the woman in the trunk, who seemed, even as they drove past the abandoned ticket counter, to have been part of the movie or part of a dream.

"You left her there?" Mona asks. "You just left?"

"We were kids."

"Plenty of kids help people in trouble," Jamila said. "Plenty of kids call 911."

"I read about a kid last week. Doused a grease fire at his mom's restaurant. Local kid."

"I had kids young as six and seven call emergency response when I was working the ED," said Doc. "You were sixteen."

"Fifteen," Brighten says. "I was fifteen."

"Fifteen's not so young."

Jamila comes up on her elbows, knees pressed out in butterfly. "What did she promise you?"

"What?"

"That woman. What did she promise you?"

"Nothing," Brighten says. "That was just Orson."

"Come on," Jamila says. "Don't tell me she never made you a promise."

Brighten is aware of having lost some control. She is not as happy as she was when she began the story. "That's what I am telling you. She never promised me anything."

"She promised him something, though. Something big. He still left her there."

"I don't see why you kept hanging around with him," Mona says, "after he pulled a stunt like that."

"He never pulled any stunt. That's the point." How to explain Orson, so they would understand? It wasn't admiration she felt that day, though she had admired his calm. It was how he behaved, as if no piece of it surprised him. How they worked in tandem, trying to help the woman. How they determined at some point, in silent agreement, that they were finished trying. Even as teenagers, they never told their parents, their other friends. The experience belonged to them, just the two of them. "We were a team," she says, though this isn't exactly right.

"You were supposed to be on her team, the woman's team," Lane says.

"We were. We were, too."

"Did she survive?" Mona asks. "The woman in the trunk?"

"I don't know," Brighten says. "How would I know?" But it seems to her, now, that she should know.

Mona laughs—a short, hard laugh.

The others are quiet. They look at each other and at their

toenails. They don't look at Brighten. When she leaves, they'll whisper about her. They'll say they can't believe she left a woman like that. They're all thinking it would have been different if they'd been there. They'd have saved her, they think. Easy, easy thoughts.

"Test your water," Doc says to Brighten. "When you get home get a match or a lighter, hold it to your faucet. If it lights, you've got methane. If it's not your husband, it's your water."

Brighten nods, but she doesn't see Doc. She sees Orson huddled over the trunk, whispering through the place where they could have wedged a coat hanger if they'd had a coat hanger. Left out, she'd wished briefly she was the one encased in the trunk.

Later, when Brighten picks Orson up at Southwestern, she tells him, "They all think you're poisoning me. The surrogates. Doc." She pitches her voice low, because Roo, who can be counted on to sleep through any drive, is napping in the rear seat.

"Doc thinks everybody's poisoned."

"This is different. She's serious."

"What do you think?"

"You remember that drive-in, years ago? Where we saw *The Towering Inferno*?"

Orson nods slowly. "I might. I guess I do."

"And the woman? The woman in the trunk."

Another slow nod.

"She promised you something. If you let her out of the trunk. What did she promise you?"

179

"I don't know. Pizza?"

"Be serious."

"It was years ago, Brighten. How should I know?" He cranks the window, so the breeze cuts between them, across anything she might say. "What does it matter? You looking to collect?"

Brighten checks Roo in the rearview, her daughter's lips quivering in the wind or from a dream. She has the sense of bringing something precious to an unconsidered end. She says, "Why didn't we help her?"

"We did. We called the police."

"No. We never did."

"There was a pay phone at the drive-in. I remember calling."

"What did they say?"

"I don't remember all that, but I know we called."

"Where is she now?"

"I don't know, Brighten."

He's impatient. Brighten can tell from his voice, his face, that he believes they called. For a moment, she allows herself to believe it as well. She sees Orson digging quarters from the crack between console and seat, sees herself on the phone, telling the dispatcher there was a woman stuck in a car, giving him the address of the Starlite Drive-in. She can see it all. She can see it perfectly. Comforting, those thoughts. She doesn't trust comfort. There beside him, she sits in a solitude that began with the surrogates and has grown steadily like the heat from a fresh flame. She leans into the wind for its coolness.

"Did it come true?"

"What?"

"Whatever she promised you."

"I told you I don't remember what she promised me."

"Maybe she promised you this."

"What? A late-night drive down a highway? Maybe she promised me Roo."

"Maybe she promised you your own land, your own truck," Brighten says. Driving home in the truck they don't own, her uterus poisoned through and useless, those things are just fantasy, as far-fetched as believing the woman in the trunk had any power at all over their lives.

"Maybe she promised me happiness," Orson says, and then they are both laughing at the absurdity of it, a promise like that.

"Maybe she promised you you'd never be trapped. Whatever happened—your work, your marriage, your kids—you'd always have a way out."

He shakes his head. "That's your wish, Brighten. Not mine."

Brighten stills as if hit by a roving spotlight, the sort they swing around in the intro to old movies, but Orson doesn't say it like it's any revelation, like it's anything to be concerned about. He taps the wheel with one hand and catches her eye, looking for her to agree. He's pleased with himself. He's pleased to have gotten it right.

Brighten feels panic—a cramp in her abdomen that forces her to take shallow breaths. Why panic? There's no immediate threat. Brighten casts around for a possible source, an understandable cause for terror. She says, "There was a moment."

"A moment?"

"When Doc asked if you were poisoning me."

Orson is quiet. "What kind of moment?"

"For a moment, I wondered." She doesn't remember wondering. She doesn't remember thinking about Orson at all. But it sounds true. It sounds possible. Why wouldn't she have wondered?

Orson nods, as if he expected even this. "You don't trust me," he says. "We should try to trust each other."

Words gentle and undemanding as a salve. She feels the fear ease, feels tender toward him for saying it, feels tender toward herself.

At home, Brighten will touch their kitchen lighter to the faucet water, letting it nod in her hand like a pumpjack until she sees, or invents, a whisker of flame, immediately extinguished. She will phone Doc to tell her, "There's methane in our water." Doc will phone the parents-to-be, and a week later the parents will send a man out to install a dispenser. For the remainder of her pregnancy, Brighten's family will drink from blue jugs like they do in the gated houses. Roo's hair will get a shine to it, and Brighten will comb it and comb it just to touch its copper sheen. Her own skin will become clear and smooth. When people attribute this to her pregnancy, she'll shake her head. "It's the water," she'll say.

She'll never get the belly she'd wanted. At thirty weeks, she'll deliver a preemie, who will spend three months in the neonatal unit in Little Rock before going home. She'll leave the hospital the day after delivery, call Doc on the way home, tell her she's not interested in doing it again. Whatever talent she had, she used it up with Roo. She won't contact the parents. They won't contact her. Occasionally, in those deep summer days, those petroleum days, she will forget the child was discharged. She'll be certain the child died, and she will briefly cry.

But before all this, as she drives home beside Orson, Roo in the rear seat, Brighten searches inside herself for the child. She listens, intently, for any knocking, any cursing, a muffled thumping against her uterus. Nothing. She imagines the small limbs drawn in tight, away from the walls of her placenta, afraid to press against that toxic flesh. She takes one hand off the wheel to find her cell phone, and she rests it on top of her stomach, plays a recording the parents sent that morning. In the background, the rhythmic whoosh of a washing machine. Over it, a voice whispers to the tissue sorting itself in her placenta, making the sort of promises no one can keep.

MANYWHERE

—

My father walks circles around my kitchen.

After twenty laps he pauses to chart his progress on a road atlas lying open beside the sink, mile by mile. He wears off-trail boots, the laces double-knotted over knee socks. His calves above his socks are bare, smooth as well-oiled pistons.

Hey, Dad, where are you walking?

He's been walking so long, he's worn through the laminate to the floorboards. From the sofa, where I write this, I can see the polished boards, the places where he's dusted the floor just by shuffling across it.

Hey, Dad, aren't you there yet?

Last time I checked his atlas, he was on the Long Trail north of Ethan's Gap, his progress charted by a trembling black line. That was days ago. By now, I'd guess he's well into Quebec. He's crossed the St. Lawrence, paused to cool his blistered feet in the river. From the bend in his back, the heel-heavy clomp of his boots, I'd bet he's walking uphill. When I stand at the stove to fry gritty-bread, he brushes past me without a word, as if I'm a tree or a fence post or an outcropping of rock, encroaching on his trail.

⤙

I'm the child he didn't choose, born to a woman he wasn't planning to marry in the summer of 1992. That year he walked the picket line, paced the pavement outside Pair-a-dice Hotel and Casino.

My mother walked with him. When they broke for lunch, he taped her feet. Taped across the top of her toes to prevent ball blisters. Layered her hot spots with benzoin and petroleum jelly. Bathed every sore with a sponge dipped not in water, which would sting the open skin, but in skim milk, pasteurized. This is the memory my mother offered when, as a child, I asked about romance. She offered it as proof of his love, but he taped the feet of everyone who walked the line. They called him Moleskin, because he always had it handy.

My mother got big with me. She got tired. She got a job at Vintage Pizza, which sat right across from the casino. Her wages paid the bills while he walked. When I was an infant, she kept me strapped in a car seat in the utility closet. When the front was slow, she sat on an upturned bleach bucket and nursed me or pumped. She kept one eye always on the picket line, where he paced back and forth.

She knew once a man starts walking, it's hard to stop him.

They didn't last. When I was four, my father walked out on her, and my mother moved in with her sister, took me along. For years, I didn't see him. We didn't speak. During those years, my father reinvented me. He made me in his image, which is to say, he made me walking. A walking daughter. One who would follow him.

He's told me about her, his walking daughter, as he rings my kitchen island. Told me she went to the University of Alabama on a soccer scholarship, led backpacking trips in the summers, studied accounting, married in her third year, never finished her fourth. Now, she has a kid and a job at the cutting table at JoAnn's, sliding a pair of snips up the shear-guide for minimum wage.

That's not true, I say to him. *That's not real.* I say this every time he brings her up. It's important to me, keeping him in check, letting him know when he's gone off into delusion or dream. I don't resent his invention of her, but I resent the life he created for her, for me—a life with no room for choice.

He's shown me photos to prove she exists. Photos of myself from three years ago, back when I still looked like a woman. Photos I can't stand to look at and certainly don't remember sharing with him. In them, I'm grinning with a toddler in my arms. *Isn't that your cousin's kid?* I ask him, but he insists it's hers. I'm posing in front of an oak's cross-section with a man I'd never choose— thick-limbed and unsmiling, a military haircut. *Is that my old co-worker?* I ask. *Her husband,* my father says.

She's not real, I tell him.

But part of me always believed in her, or wanted to believe. I waited for her like a banana spider hung between two leaves. I kept a full set of my old clothes for her. I kept beer and cigarettes in the cabinet above the fridge, because he said those were her go-tos. I prepared to hand him off to her. I'd been living six months with my father. It was her turn.

I used to wonder if I'd seen her. Bodysurfing in the bay. Buying scallops at the Publix seafood counter. I once bummed a cigarette and a maxi pad off someone in a CVS parking lot who might have been her.

Then, three days ago, I met her.

I saw her sitting at the bar inside Sandshaker, a backpack leaning against her stool. She was sipping a margarita through a straw. I slid in. I bought her a drink.

She said, *I'm married.*

I said, *I know.*

We looked similar, same eyes, same pebbling of acne scars on our jaw. She didn't mention this, so neither did I. I didn't ask about the specifics of her life. I had no desire to hear them confirmed.

Instead I asked, *Did you walk here?*

I've been walking fifty days, she said. *Big Cypress to Blackwater, loneliest through-hike in America.*

I decided, then, it was her.

When they called close, I took up her backpack, led her out into the parking lot, offered for her to sleep over at my apartment on the peninsula, offered to give her a ride in the morning to whatever trailhead struck her fancy.

Rides are cheating, she said, but she was tempted. It was late, and the mosquitoes sang a cloud over our heads, and she was tipsy enough to be responsive to suggestion.

I want to show you my home, I told her then. *There's someone I want you to meet.*

When I was old enough and we were talking again, my father took me walking. We walked pieces of the Appalachian Trail, Old Rag Mountain, Hawksbill Peak.

Every night I spent with him I spent under the stars. Now I think it's because he didn't have another place. He was sleeping on friends' couches and in spare bedrooms at the time, places where bringing a kid home might stretch hospitality to a breaking point. Back then, I believed it romantic, believed him an adventurer.

Nobody'll thank you for walking, he told me once. *Walking's its own reward.*

As we walked, he told me of the places he'd seen. His many-wheres. Never what he'd done, whom he'd met, whom he'd loved. Only where he'd been.

He'd learned to walk in Miami. He was seventeen. He'd left home or run from home. He was a slope walker. He learned to point his toes to the waves to compensate for the slant of the land. Walking the beaches. Working the beaches. When he was twenty-six, he left South Florida, walked though the cypress swamp, across the palm flats, from Apalachicola out along Highway 98, because a buddy of his had a job for him at Pair-a-dice. He says he got there two weeks later in the best shape of his life.

This can't be true. I've mapped it out. Even walking twenty miles a day, it would have taken him more than a month. But I never confronted him, never asked for the truth. It's important to me, maintaining some image of him as wanderer. I want to believe my father the sort of man who'd stop everything to watch a pair of snakes fuck in the sand. Gentle that way.

After his first shift at Pair-a-dice, he went to some greasy dive, and the barback eyed his earring. *These illegal up here?* my father asked, fingers on the gold hoop.

Two types wear those, the barback said. *Bikers and fags. Both cause trouble.* My father removed his earring, left it on the counter beside a sizable tip.

When the workers went on strike, he held the line at Pair-a-dice, kept scabs and customers alike from crossing. He threw bricks. He punched a man who crossed to gamble. He was arrested for assault. As a teenager, I asked him about it. He shook his head. *I only held him*, he said. *Another man swung.* I told him, *That's not any better.* He said he was sorry, and he looked sorry. He wanted me to think well of him. He worried I didn't like him, and often I didn't.

He taught me things—how to hunt shelf fungus, how to anchor a rappelling line to a tree. We had rituals. At the end of a day of walking, he'd lead me off-trail, deep into whatever hammock or marsh bordered the footpath, and tie a sweaty T-shirt over my eyes. He spun me by the shoulders until I was so dizzy I stumbled, then asked, *Which way are you facing?* I had to guess the direction correctly and find my way back to the trail. If I failed at either test, we began again. Only after I'd completed both could we sleep. Some nights it took six tries, or ten. *I'm tired*, he'd say then. *Aren't you ready for sleep?* He'd curse the dusk and my slowness. *Hurry, so we can sleep.* Sometimes, I failed and slept with my eyes covered in the duff on the edge of the trail.

We got caught in a mudslide in Goat Basin. The left bank shivered, rippled like a great muscle and fell. We ran from the mud. Uphill. You don't know how hard you can run until you're there and you're running. When the slide had settled we turned back to look. The mud was gritty like cornmeal. We went through it. I lost my boot. He lost his hiking poles. We walked where we could on trees uprooted and tangled like a great mat of hair. He hadn't brought a jacket. His face went gray and slack around the jaw, his lips also gray. I offered him my jacket.

You sure? he said.

I'm fine, I said. *I'll be fine.* He took it, and I felt a surge of disappointment. He looked ridiculous. My jacket over his shoulders— too short, too small.

When we got to the far side of the basin, rangers wrapped us in space blankets and gave us warm water and told us we were idiots to go through the basin. We should have gone up the ridge, and if we'd known anything at all we'd have known that. But we were giddy—high on adrenaline and our own survival. *I'd like to be a ranger*, my father said to the rangers, and I laughed at the faces they made, all taken aback. I laughed at how he looked in my jacket and kept on like that laughing until the warmth and the pain came back and, briefly, I loved him.

We made for the nearest campground afterward, to resupply. There, we met his buddy and abandoned our tent for a space in his RV, which had heat and a microwave and a television with eight channels. Looking back, this must all have been planned, but at the time I believed it some fortunate, almost unbelievable serendipity.

His buddy painted tires—his own tires and other people's tires, tractor tires and flat tires. The RV was hung with dozens of half-finished canvases. When he ran out of space, he burned the oldest canvases for kindling.

In the night, my father left me lying on the bed in the RV while they drank together. They left the camp. I know, because I checked. I imagined long, starlit hikes. I imagined sex. I lay, unsleeping, in the loft bed and said my father's full name—John Leroy Vickers—over and over, a summoning, until he returned.

Tell me, where were you walking?

His buddy sometimes sold his paintings to tourists in the neighboring sites. This was illegal, but mostly no one cared. The only ticket he ever got came from a woman ranger with a hat beaten in on the top.

My father said, as the ranger pulled away in her golf cart, *She comes by again, you know what I'd do? I'd put new sheets on the bed and invite her inside.*

His buddy laughed. Embarrassed. *Come on, Roy.*

You could have a turn with her. It's your RV.

Come on. Looking at me. *Charlotte's right here. What about Charlotte?*

Charlie? My father was quiet a moment. As usual, I puzzled him. *Want to drive the golf cart, Charlie?* he asked eventually.

Sure, I said. I was fourteen. I'd have driven anything.

There you go, he said. *Charlie will get rid of her golf cart.*

After a week of this, of the two of them, I hitched out of the park. Got money from my mother for a stand-by flight home to Tampa. A day later, I heard my mother talking to my father on the phone. In her voice a hard, bitter pleasure—*Guess she got tired of being one of the guys.*

But I wasn't bothered then by his water-stained socks or the way he fried just the whites of eggs, left the yolks to congeal in their half shells—a patience I wish I still had.

I always sent him my addresses. Six months in Pensacola. Four in Atlanta. A two-year stint in Orlando for school. I liked to think they cheered him, that he took comfort in my vagrancy, thought I took after him. I never expected he'd come find me, but he did. Six months ago, he knocked on the door of the apartment in Perdido I was sharing with a woman who was sometimes my partner and sometimes my friend. *I could use a place for a few nights*, he said.

He stayed. We had a foldout futon. He had nowhere else to go. It was then he started the walking. Round and round in our kitchen.

I was working for the conservation corps, clearing air potatoes from the hardwood forests. The woman living with me worked at home, so she was the one who offered to fry my father an egg when he'd walked six miles without pausing for a meal.

I'd text her during the day, checking up on her and on him, supporting her how I could, my thumbs sliding sweaty over the screen of my phone. One day, she didn't answer. Six texts I sent her that morning. I called her—a last resort, we never called. Nothing.

I called the police. I told them he'd been transient, once been arrested for assault. I told them he was there with her, just the two of them in that apartment.

When they arrived, she was working in her office, her phone

silenced in the bedroom. He was walking. Both of them were flustered by the officers' questions.

What did you think had happened? he asked me when I got home.

I got nervous, I said. *Haven't you ever been nervous like that for someone?*

She asked me, *Am I safe here?*

I said, *Of course you are. Of course you're safe.*

I thought she'd leave then, but she didn't. She left four months later, tired of the beat of his walking, tired of finding his orange peels decomposing in the pot of our fiddle-leaf fig. The day she left, she said, *I can't live this way.*

I said, *I understand,* but I thought it was a cruel thing, a thing better left unsaid—that she found my life unbearable. *I can't either,* I said.

She gave me a look then, like I was failing to make some difficult, necessary choice. I don't see any choice but the choice I'm living, not until I convince someone to take my place. I tried once, leaving him. I went rafting with friends on the Tennessee. When I got home a week later he was lying between the oven and the kitchen island, his left leg bent underneath him. *Hit a patch of ice,* he said. *How long ago?* I asked him, but he couldn't remember. He said he was fine, and he was in a sense—nothing broken, not dead. But when I helped him up, when he straightened the leg that had been bent beneath him for hours or maybe for days, he screamed.

I spend my days back in my bedroom, the only room in the house that still feels like mine. I live on canned chowder and crackers, pee into a big ceramic vase that used to hold the fiddle-leaf fig. I check on him once a day to ensure he's eaten, to check he's still walking. When I emerge, he talks to me. He says things he wants me to know. *I think women are beautiful*, he says. *I always thought your mother was beautiful.*

He watches me as he says these things, judging my reaction. *You understand me?* he says. *You'd be a beautiful woman. I don't see why you don't want to be a woman.*

You think you can slip through some sort of loophole, he tried on another occasion. *Not choose either way.*

I've considered, of course, that it might be cowardice. A refusal to decide anything, even gender—further evidence of my deep and abiding ambivalence.

He's since found reasoning he likes better: *You don't want to be like your mother.*

I tell him it's older than that. It's older than I am. It's someone in his line, some great-great-grandparent caught out alone in uncertain terrain, days from any familiar shelter, walking up to a men's bunkhouse with their hair shorn and their boots muddy, hoping to pass so hard the hope got lodged in the blood, passed down through him to me.

I never gave a damn about those things. Fitting in with other guys. Any of that.

You did. After that mudslide you did. You said you wanted to be a ranger.

I never did.

You just don't remember. You don't remember where the forks are in this kitchen you've lived in for six months.

It's not worth my time, remembering things like that.

You couldn't if you wanted to.

Sure I could.

Where are the forks? Which drawer?

You sound like your mother.

Where?

He looked knob to knob like a deer caught midriver, and I said, *Never mind. It doesn't matter.*

He went to each drawer, opening and shutting them until he found the forks. He didn't make any show of finding them, just shut the drawer and started up walking again. I sat there, awash in my pettiness, understanding if I weren't careful I could become this person not for an evening but for my entire life. Later he said, *Getting old doesn't scare me.*

I said, *Well, it terrifies me,* meaning not him but that person I could become, nagging and cruel.

I leave the front door open in the evenings. *For a breeze,* I tell him, but I'm also hoping to tempt him out or his supposed daughter in. When I've had enough of talking to him, I go into my bedroom and undress and lie on the bed, eyes shut, my head pulsing with heat and restlessness. I thought once—I didn't go looking for the thought, it just came—that I would do anything for a month to myself, and I felt the weight of it, that word *anything.*

People like to tell you to walk away. They like to think you're freer than you are. I can't leave him. I can't afford any sort of home for him, and he's got nobody else, nobody except, maybe, her.

In the Sandshaker the night I met her, I excused myself. I shut myself in the one-toilet bathroom and called him. I told him I'd found her. *Your daughter*, I said on the phone. *She's here.* What did I expect him to do? Come and get her? Maybe. Maybe I wanted to believe he'd do that for her, for me. *Who?* he said. *Who?*

Your daughter, I said.

I'm talking to my daughter, he said.

No, I said.

Then who am I talking to?

I hung up.

I convinced her to walk the half mile home with me. *It's so beautiful*, she said, of the black water lapping at the road we walked, chewing the asphalt away, so cars had to swerve to the middle or risk running off into the Gulf. *You're so lucky to live here.*

You could live here, too.

When we got to the apartment, she kicked off her boots and stepped right inside. I expected her to be wary after months on the trail, but the opposite seemed true. She'd dined and lodged with strangers. She was tame like a fat park squirrel, didn't question hospitality. In this way, she reminded me of him.

I brought someone for you, I told him when we entered.

Who's that? he said from the kitchen.

Charlotte, she said.

Charlotte, he said. Did he recognize her? I couldn't tell. He paused in his loop to shake her hand, said, *Where you coming from?*

She's walking, I said. *The Florida Trail.*

She complimented the softness of the carpet and my screen print of Medusa in a strap-on, and the laminate countertops, and even the sleeping mask he wore, which was crumpled on the futon. *Wish I could afford an apartment like this.*

When she said it, I felt a new urgency. She'd given me a signal. She was telling me I could make this happen if I played it right. Even if she wasn't really his daughter, maybe she'd consent to stay.

I opened a beer for her, because beer stalls any traveler. I made her chamomile tea. I pulled tofu from the fridge, almonds from the cabinets, foods to set you dreaming. When she asked how she could help, which most women will, I gave her home-making tasks. She spent fifteen minutes sweeping sand from the back porch. When she finished, I asked her to repaint the trim around the door an eggshell white.

How's your family? he asked while she painted. He was solicitous of her, happy to see her.

They're all right. Get on me about being gone too long.

They got onto me the same way. Don't let it bother you.

She caught sight of the atlas and asked him about it, and they were off together. She walked his loop behind him, dripping paint on the floor as they talked about the different routes up Half Dome, the perils of snow bridges. I almost envied her ease.

She said, *I wish my dad had taught me all this.*

You can see how I came to think of it as a gift on both sides— her staying, me leaving.

Walking keeps me young, he said. *Keeps me limber.*

I can see that, she said.

He only walks here, I said. *Round the kitchen.*

I thought we might share some humor at this, but *That's neat*, she said. *My cousin takes vacations on his maps app. Went all over Spain that way. Virtual.*

The way she said that—*virtual*—made me realize she was young. I reminded myself I was young, too.

How's your feet? he asked her.

They're okay.

Let's see them.

I don't know.

Let's see.

She climbed up onto the counter beside the sink. Her socks were splotched brown, and she tugged the first one down slowly, wincing as it peeled off the heel.

Hurts less if you take it off quick, he said. He took her other sock between his fingers and yanked. It came away inside out, stiff, holding the shape of her foot. Her skin beneath the socks was a mess of hot spots. She had blisters on both of her pinky toes. He shook his head. He took her ankles in his hands one at a time, noting the troubled areas, his manner clinical, professional.

These won't last you a week.

She squirmed, embarrassed, like she regretted all of this. I reminded her about her beer, and she drank from it for courage.

I took her socks. I said, *I'll get these in the washer.*

Don't. Don't worry about it, she said. She reached out her hand for them.

It's no hassle, I said. *Socks this dirty, you're sure to blister.* I didn't have laundry of my own to do, so I stopped at her pack on my way to the washer. It was full of clothing that hadn't seen soap in days. I loaded the washer up with as much as it could take, added two full caps of detergent—scent-free in case she had allergies.

When I returned he had his moleskin, his petroleum jelly, and his antibiotic ointment set out on the counter, a little parade of foot care products. He had a needle in his hand and was draining the blisters, telling her as he did it, *I went across Walker Glacier, up in Alaska, before it disappeared.*

Usually I would have corrected him, insisted he only imagined that hike, but she nodded along with him, so I let it go.

I was born too late for glacier hiking, she said.

By the time her feet were taped and oiled, I'd confirmed she had no allergies and made a dish of almond-encrusted tofu, which we ate standing in the kitchen. *We could teach you things,* I told her as we passed the peppercorn person to person like a family. *We could teach you this game we played when we were hiking.* I looked at him, willing him to help me. *You remember?*

He walked a few steps away from his plate and back to it. *Sure, I remember.*

What's the game? she said.

It's a navigation game. One of us spins around, then we have to guess which way we're facing.

You loved that game, he said to me, which I did not contest.

Want to play? I asked her.

She fingered the ends of her hair, and I recalculated. Too quick. Too forward. I felt the desperate, grasping feeling I felt sometimes on dates, when it was clear the other person was just waiting for a lag, a pause, a space to exit.

After dinner, I said.

Sure, maybe. But when she'd finished eating, she said, *I think I'll walk a ways more tonight.*

You just got here, he said. *You can't take off yet.*

I've got a bed made up for you, I said.

It's time I get going.

Your socks are in the washer.

I've got another pair.

I shook my head. *I tossed it all in the washer. I'm sorry. I thought you were staying.*

She left the kitchen to get her pack, and when she brought it back, half-empty, she was different—tighter, alert. *I need my stuff.*

It just needs to dry. We can hang it right now to dry.

We took her bundle of clothes from the washer onto the second-story porch, where a clotheshorse and three short lines were waiting. *Do you like it here?* I asked, as I stretched a pair of nylon pants across the rack.

I like the marsh, she said. *I'm not in any hurry to finish the trail.*

Maybe you don't have to finish it.

You mean I could make myself a loop? she said. She laughed, nervous but easier now that she had her clothes in front of her. We laughed together. A good sign.

You could live here, I said.

Here? She laughed, again. Alone.

You're good with him, I told her. *Better than I am. We've been in the same space too long, just get on each other's nerves.*

I've got a kid. I've got a husband.

It's just me and him all the time. I can't stand it.

She pinned a pair of knit boy-cuts to the line.

I can't stand him.

Leave, then, she said.

Someone has to stay with him.

I don't understand.

He doesn't have any friends. He's an old man. He can't live alone. I pulled a burr from the cuff of one wool sock. *It's your turn.*

My turn?

Probably, she wasn't his daughter. Probably, she had no relation to either one of us. I had long since stopped caring about that. One thing mattered: that she remain and I leave. *You have to stay.*

I'd frightened her, a little, but there it was said. The worst over, and she hadn't yelled. She wasn't wide-eyed. She hadn't run. She stood holding a silk undershirt to her chest, the sleeves dripping onto her feet, looking at me like she was waiting for a punch line.

I've got this, she said finally, motioning to the pile of not-yet-hung clothes. *You don't need to help me.*

Okay, I said. *I'll get the game ready for us.* I turned to go into the kitchen, but when I tried to open the door, it bounced back at me. My father's boot was right there. He was standing just behind it.

What are you doing? I hissed, stepping inside and shutting the door behind me. *I thought you were walking.*

Voices carry, you know that? I heard all you said. An old man. Just an old man.

You are *an old man.* I ducked past him into the closet where I kept old T-shirts for rags, searching for one that was long enough to wrap around a head and tie.

He followed, stood behind me. *You're tired of me, you could say so. You could say it to my face.*

I'm trying to do you a favor.

You don't want to live with me anymore, I'll go.

Where? Where would you go?

You don't need to worry about that.

I do worry about it. You don't have anywhere.

I have lots of places.

I couldn't find a T-shirt, but I saw his mask then, twisted on the futon. *This'll work.*

For what?

For the game. Has everyone but me forgotten about the game?

I'm not as bad off as you think I am, he said.

The door slammed, then, the back door, and I cursed and took off. She wasn't in the kitchen, and her bag wasn't in the kitchen, and I threw the switch for the back porch lights, thinking we'd lost her, but when the lights snapped on, she froze—on the back porch, neck twisted into the light, shadow splayed, insect-like, on the half wall behind her. We watched her. We made no sound, and after a time, as a buck grows accustomed to the glow of a porch light triggered by its movement, she returned to her pack. She pulled her wet clothes off the line, shoved them inside. She put her heavy, soggy pack up onto the half wall. There was no way off the back porch except to jump and drop a dozen feet into the hedge beneath. She pushed her pack over the edge of the wall and that's when I opened the door, casual, to keep her from doing anything she'd later regret, any desperate, harmful thing. *You taking off?* I said.

I think I'd better.

I dangled the sleeping mask from my fingers and smiled what I hoped was an easy, friendly smile. *One game before you go.*

Hamstrung by politeness or realizing she was trapped, she agreed.

In the living room, I put the mask on her, tied a knot in the elastic to keep it tight, working carefully so I wouldn't catch and pull her hair. He'd gone around back for her pack and now stood by the front door, pulling her wet clothes from the top one by one, laying them out on the futon as if to dry them right there.

She was shaking a little. *My husband's expecting me home*, she said. *He'll come looking for me if I don't show up home.*

He's welcome here, I said. *You tell him I said that.*

I spun her by her shoulders, and for a single wild second I thought I could spin her forever, could pause all of us in our various trajectories. Then the moment passed, and her spinning slowed. *The game ends when you find your bed for the night*, I told her. I kept my hands on her shoulders until she found her feet, then let her go.

Where's your bed? I said, and my father joined in, both of us chanting as she extended her arms and felt her way forward. *Where's your bed? Where's your bed?* Her shin hit the coffee table, and she cursed, but she kept on. For a few minutes, she said nothing, and I worried she'd get frustrated, but then she found the doorway she'd painted, put her hand on it, her fingers coming away tacky with fresh white paint, and she crowed, *I'm facing the kitchen. I'm facing the ocean.*

We cheered. She was right. After that, I think she enjoyed

herself, exploring the hallway, her fingers leaving little white prints on the futon cover, a trail of white paint down the wall. She shouted, *Am I close? Am I closer?* as she made her way into the bathroom. She left her mark on the mirror and the taps, more confident now, and soon she was standing at the foot of the bed that had been mine. She leaned on it, ran her hands up the comforter to the pillows. *This one. This one's mine.* She said it triumphantly. She knew she was right.

This is it, I said. *This is yours.* She took off the mask. I turned the bed down for her, felt a premature nostalgia for the bulky lumpy comforter, the sheets with small flowers. She bounced on the edge of the mattress, nervous or maybe just testing the springs. *You need anything else?*

No, she said.

I'll see you in the morning, I said.

You're not staying?

It's too cozy for two.

I thought you were staying.

I'll be just outside. I gave her a moment. *You change your mind about sleeping here?*

No, she said. *I don't have much choice at this point, do I?* Angry. She was angry, but at herself I think, not at me.

In the kitchen, where my father was walking late to compensate for the hours lost to conversation, I filled my own pack. I half expected he would stop me. Maybe I wanted him to. But he was looking into the distance, wandering through some Canadian wild. I left my keys on the island, and I walked through the front door, heard it click shut and lock behind me. I felt how suddenly it could happen, this becoming an outsider. Already, to reenter the apartment, I'd have to ask permission.

I walked with purpose, as if I had some bus or plane to catch, but I didn't have anything to catch, didn't have anyone waiting for me except in that house behind me. I walked with no destination, navigating by the sound of the incoming tide, the dune grass flattened for me by the last person who'd walked there.

Notes

—

10 Quotations assembled from "She Posed as a Man for Fifteen Years" (*New York Times*, Oct. 5, 1908); "Woman in Male Garb Gains Her Freedom" (*New York Times*, Oct. 6, 1908); "Mustached, She Plays Man" (*New York Sun*, Oct. 5, 1908); "Passed Off as a Man" (*Washington [D.C.] Evening Star*, Oct. 5, 1908); "Lived 15 Years as a Man" (*New York Daily Tribune*, Oct. 5, 1908); "Women Who Have Lived as Men" (*Herald Democrat*, Jan. 26, 1901).

19 "Lightning goes through and through a man but only peels a tree," from "The Lightning-Rod Man," by Herman Melville (1854).

41 Descriptions of anorexia from *On Visceral Neuroses* by T. C. Allbutt (Delivered at the Royal College of Physicians in March, 1884), "On Hysterical Anorexia" by E. Ch. Lasègue (*Archives Générales de Médecine*, 1873), "Anorexia Nervosa" by W. W. Gull (*Lancet*, 1888), and "Anorexia Nervosa and the Insula" by K. Nunn (*Science*, 2010).

59 Court transcript adapted from the testimony of Thomas/ine Hall (*Minutes of the Council and General Court of Colonial Virginia*, 1629).

64 "It pleased the Lord, seven weeks after we arrived in this country . . . without her society and assistance," from the letter of Reverend Jonas Michäelius (from *Manhattan in 1628*).

140 Doctors' quotes from "Infant Mortality in South Carolina" by W. E. Simpson (*Journal of South Carolina Medical Association*, 1928); "Discussion on the Midwife" by W. R. Nicholson (appeared in "The Midwife, Society Proceedings: American Association for Study and Prevention of Infant Mortality," *Journal of the American Medical Association*, 1916); and

"Ignorance, Superstition, Quackery" by R. B. Furman (*Journal of South Carolina Medical Association*, 1916).

143 Elizabeth's journal entry adapted from "An Open Air Class" by Ruth Dodd (*The Public Health Nurse*, 1921).

146 "The mammies' nails are dirty, their hands indescribable" adapted from "Rat Pie" by C. C. Van Blarcom (*Harper's Magazine*, 1930).

155 Testimony informed by *Birth Behind the Veil: African American Midwives and Mothers in the Rural South, 1921–1962* by Kelena Reid Maxwell (dissertation submitted to Rutgers University, 2009).

Acknowledgments

—

These stories were written on the occupied lands of the Chinook, Osage, and Muscogee nations. Acknowledgment, first, to the people of those nations, and thanks to my colleagues Jessica Leston and Itai Jeffries for holding space for me to complete this book while also working to navigate my accountability as settler.

Thanks to my fierce and discerning agent, Meredith Kaffel Simonoff, and to everyone at Defiore & Company, especially Jacey Mitziga. To Jackson Howard for his insightful editing and his championing of this book, and to everyone at MCD/FSG, especially Chloe Texier-Rose and Janine Barlow. To Meredith Talusan, for connecting me with my editor.

Thanks to my dazzling and brilliant friends, who read these stories in their earliest forms: Charlie Schneider, 'Pemi Aguda, Daphne Andreades, and Rose Lambert-Sluder.

Thanks to my teachers Marjorie Celona, Cai Emmons, Jason Brown, Kelly Link, Tania James, and Siamak Vossoughi, for your patience and guidance. Last, and especially, to Mary Robison, that earliest teacher, for your faith in me.

A NOTE ABOUT THE AUTHOR

Morgan Thomas's work has appeared in *The Atlantic*, the *Kenyon Review*, *American Short Fiction*, *The Yale Review*, *Electric Literature*, and *Story Quarterly*, where their story won the 2019 Fiction Prize. They are the recipient of a Bread Loaf Work-Study Grant, a Fulbright Grant, the Penny Wilkes Scholarship in Writing and the Environment, and the inaugural Southern Studies Fellowship in Arts and Letters. They have also received fellowships from the Sewanee Writers' Conference and the Arctic Circle. A graduate of the University of Oregon MFA program, they live in Portland.